D1457538

MUST LOVE

MUST LOVE HOCKEY

SARINA BOWEN

Tuxbury Publishing LLC

CHAPTER ONE

NINETEEN THOUSAND MINUS ONE

1

Emily

"Come on, Brooklyn!" I shriek. "Let's do this!"

Charles—my boyfriend—gives me a sideways glance. It's a look that says I'm being a little louder than he likes.

But *come on*. We're at a hockey game, and it's tied 2-2 with only five minutes on the clock. Now is not the time to be the demure corporate girlfriend. His clients don't care, anyway. They're all enjoying themselves tremendously.

It's a Wednesday night, and I have class at eight a.m. tomorrow. I shouldn't even be here. But I love hockey. "Get there!" I scream as Mark "Tank" Tankiewicz lunges for the puck.

This earns me another sideways glance from Charles.

But I ignore him. Two or three nights a week, he asks me to accompany him to client events. He's twenty-two, only a year older than I am. But while I'm still in college, he's already an analyst for the high-net-worth division at Merrill Lynch. This outing is part of his job. And he takes his job very seriously.

When Charles was interviewing for the position, we had no idea that it would include all these nights out with clients. Who knew rich people like to be entertained by the people who manage their money? Or by the people who get coffee for the people who manage their money. Charles is barely more than a trainee, but he's very ambitious.

"Charles will run the world someday," my mother loves to say. She's probably right. In her next breath, she always adds: "And he needs a good woman at his side."

My mother and Charles are on the same wavelength. I'm not sure why it annoys me so much. But either Charles really is God's gift to humanity, or she just appreciates the fact that I found a nice, respectable man. The fact that he's also Asian American is just a bonus.

In fact, there are days when I'm sure Mom likes Charles more than she likes me. Quite a few of them.

But none of that matters right now, because Brooklyn has the puck again, and I want this win. I lean forward in my seat, as if I could somehow affect the game from way up here in row Q. *One more goal!* My palms actually itch from clenching my hands.

Now Crikey has the puck. He stick-handles it past the defender. "Come on!" I shriek. "Let's do this!"

I hold my breath as he fakes a pass to Wilson and then slots the puck to Castro, instead.

"Shoot!" I scream.

"Emily," Charles hisses. "My ears!"

Castro fires back to Wilson, who shoots so fast I can barely register the movement. The lamp lights. Nineteen thousand people stand up and scream.

Well, nineteen thousand minus one. Charles doesn't scream. Not even at a hockey game. But the rest of us are on our feet. The tie has been broken, and three minutes from now, Brooklyn is bound to be the winner.

"No Sleep till Brooklyn" comes blaring through the speakers, and I wiggle my butt in time with the music. I catch Charles looking at me like I might have lost my mind. "What?" I demand. "We're at a hockey game."

He just shakes his head.

Deflated, I sit back down beside him. My hands are tingling. It's weird. My palms are still itchy. When I inspect them, there's some redness, but it isn't very dramatic. I reach for my soda and find it completely empty.

Heck. When did I drain that? And why am I so thirsty?

"Where shall we go for drinks after the game?" Charles asks his two clients and their wives.

"How about Stokers in Alphabet City?" one of the guys says. "That place cracks me up."

Crap. I really don't need to go into Manhattan on a school night.

"Sounds great," Charles says, ever the pleaser.

I watch three more minutes of hockey and try to craft my sorry-I've-got-to-go-home speech. I live deeper into Brooklyn than where we are right now. Stokers is in exactly the wrong direction.

The clock runs down, and loud, happy music starts playing again right after the buzzer. All the fans are on their feet, this time grabbing their coats. I put mine on, too. We're up pretty high in the stands and getting out of here is going to be slow work. We won't get to the bar until almost midnight.

I really can't go.

"Come out with us," Charles whispers to me, as if reading my thoughts. "I'll make it up to you." His brown eyes search mine.

"You can't make up a lost night's sleep," I whisper.

"It will all get easier soon," he murmurs. "I'll get a place in the city."

He wants to move to Manhattan, and he wants me to move in with him. I think there's also a wedding ring in this scenario. I haven't asked for more details, because I'm not sure I'm ready for that.

Charles is on his phone at the moment, though, summoning a hired car to take the four of us to Manhattan and taking my elbow as we start moving toward the exit. "Just one drink," he whispers to me. "Then you can Uber home."

He knows I should go home and go to bed. In fact, he should, too.

But, nope. What the client wants, the client gets.

The crowd begins to file into the aisles, inching slowly toward the exits. I rub my tingling palms together and try not to feel irritated.

It doesn't work. In fact, it gets worse. It takes almost thirty minutes until we reach the cool, outdoor air. And it will take at least thirty more to get to the bar in post-game traffic.

"Have a great night!" says a smiling Ice Girl from just inside the front door. She's wearing a furry cropped jacket in Brooklyn's team color, and tight black jeans and heels.

Charles eyes her butt as we walk by. And I can't even gather up enough energy to feel angry about it, because I'm not doing so well. I feel a little dizzy. My heart is racing, and I'm breathing too fast. And then there's the weird little itch that's starting in my throat.

Maybe I'm having a panic attack. That happens once in a while.

As our group rounds the corner of the stadium, I fall back. I lean against the exterior wall and try to take a deep, slow breath. Something's wrong with me.

"Emily!" Charles barks. He whips around, scanning the crowd. When he finally spots me against the wall, he frowns. "What's the matter? Why can't you keep up?"

The clients and their wives turn their heads, and now everyone is staring at me. "I'm tired," I croak. "I'd better go home."

Charles reaches me in three urgent strides. "Emily, this is embarrassing."

Now my eyes feel hot. "Charles, I don't feel well. Go without me."

"Are you nauseated?" He squints at me.

"No, I just feel..." I swallow, and my throat is unnaturally thick. "*Weird*."

Charles rolls his eyes. "I gotta go, Emily. Seriously. They're waiting."

"Go on, then," I rasp.

He leans in, pecks me on the cheek and then turns and strides off.

The others are still staring at me. I give them a tired wave and a half smile. I just want to be alone right now.

Finally, they're gone. I breathe a deep sigh of relief. Or rather, I try to. My breathing still feels shallow. Heck, I need to get home. I squint, looking around for the subway entrance. I push off the wall and walk slowly toward the corner of Dean Street, sticking close to the building. It's not very far, but I feel winded. The familiar green signs for the subway are another half block away, but they're labeled for the 2 and 3 trains.

I need the B or Q. *Crap.*

And I feel…awful. I prop a hand against the stadium wall to shore myself up while I try to catch my breath. Slowly, I move around the corner of the building. I know there's another subway entrance around here, because I checked the map earlier today.

But I have to separate from my new best friend—the nice, cool wall—as I approach what must be the stadium's loading dock. The doors are open, and there're a couple guys carrying gear from the building and loading it onto a van.

One of them stops what he's doing to watch me. Any other night I would stare at him, because he's seriously cute—with big, dark eyes and a tight-fitting Brooklyn Bruisers shirt stretched across an incredible chest. But at the moment, he's just in my way. I steer my body toward the front of the van, so I won't interrupt his work.

"Hey, miss?" he calls after me. "Are you okay?"

I open my mouth, but only a squeak comes out. "Yes?" The Brooklyn lights shimmer around me, and I close my eyes to try to focus on getting home.

When I open them again, he's come closer. "You don't look okay. Can I help you? Grab you a taxi, maybe?" The voice is so polite, especially in contrast with the badass, muscular body standing in front of me.

"Okay," I rasp, because even though I can't afford a taxi, I feel too woozy to navigate the subway.

"Why are you pulling on your collar?" he asks, tilting his head to the side.

I drop my hand, because I hadn't realized I was. "My throat is…" I swallow. "It's a little hard to breathe." Even as I say these words, fear slides down my spine. Something is wrong, and I don't know how to make it right.

"Come inside for a second," he says gently, touching my arm to steer me toward the loading bay. "The light isn't very good here. But I think you've got spots on your throat."

"Spots?" I gasp. I push my hand into my bag to try to fish out my phone. The zipper catches my sleeve, pushing it up my forearm. I raise my hand and stare in disbelief. There are bright red spots on my inner arm. I can only gape at them in terror.

"Holy cannelloni," he says. "Come with me."

CHAPTER TWO

MAKE IT
STOP

2

James

This girl is not okay. She's impeccably dressed in a sweater, a skirt, stockings, and shiny shoes. She's wearing a wool coat and pearl earrings. At some point earlier today, she was probably doing just fine. But she practically staggered around the corner of the building.

At first, I thought she might just be drunk. But drunk women don't breathe funny. And they don't have hives all over their neck and wrists. Those spots—bright red blotches against her smooth, golden-hued skin—look angry.

Something is very wrong, and her dark eyes look frightened.

As quickly as she can manage, I lead her through the loading dock and down a ramp toward the locker rooms. There's a security guard waiting outside the locker room complex. He cocks an eyebrow as I approach with a stranger.

"Rudy, did you see Doc leave?" I ask.

Rudy shrugs. "Go on in and check." He holds the door open.

"What's your name?" I ask the ailing young woman on my arm. She's holding on for dear life.

"Emily Chen," she gasps.

"Nice to meet you, Emily. I'm James, but everyone calls me Jimbo. I want to see if Doc Herberts is still here, okay? Sit." I lower her onto a bench in the outer locker area, where the players keep their coats and street shoes.

Most of the players are gone already, but Anton Bayer gives me a curious glance as he shrugs his coat on. "You okay, Jimbo?"

"I need Doc. Is he still here?"

Bayer winces. "I feel like I saw him bolt out of here. There's a train he likes to catch if nobody is bleeding."

Shit. I pull out my phone and hit his number.

Luckily, he answers right away. "This is Herberts. Jimbo? Is there a problem?"

"Hey Doc—what does a bad allergic reaction look like? I have a fan here with hives and shallow breathing."

"Slow down, kid. Can I talk to him?"

"Her," I correct. "Her name is Emily. I'm putting you on speaker." I hit the button and hold the phone near Emily. She looks panicked.

"Hi, Emily," Doc's voice says. "I hear you're having some trouble. Can you describe it?"

"I was fine for most of the game," she wheezes. "But then my palms felt tingly. And my throat itches."

"Do you have any food allergies?" Doc asks.

"No." She gives her head a shake. "Never."

"She has hives," I break in. "On her wrists. And I see them on her neck." I give her collar a little tug, and Emily's eyes widen. "Hey, I'm sorry," I babble. "But they're really bright now."

"Send me a photo, Jimbo. And Emily," Doc asks. "Do you feel any swelling, especially in your mouth?"

She puts a hand to her face. "My lips. It's so weird." She drops her hand to her sweater and pulls the turtleneck away from her skin. "I'm scared. It's hard to breathe."

"Jimbo, are her lips blue?"

I squint. Usually when I'm staring at a pretty girl's lips, it's not for this. "Maybe?" I say, wishing I knew how Emily's lips are supposed to look.

"But I have lipstick on," she wheezes.

Well, fuck. "What do I do, Doc?"

"The best course of action is an emergency room," he says. "But—"

"It's carmaggedon outside the stadium!" I explode. We'd be lucky to get to an ER in under an hour, unless I carry Emily down the subway steps. She doesn't look like she could make it.

"I know, son," he says. "I'm thinking. She should really be seen by a professional. But if I were there, I'd probably administer epinephrine. If she's going into anaphylactic shock, that would stop it. And even if she isn't, the odds of it harming her are pretty low."

"Okay. So—"

"If Wilson is still around, he can get one of the EpiSticks we keep on hand for him."

"Oh, *right*." I should have already thought of Wilson and his tree-nut allergy. "WILSON!" I holler toward the dressing room.

The door opens. "Who needs Wilson?" It's Leo Trevi. "You sound like Tom Hanks in that *Cast Away* movie."

"*Omigosh ish Leo Trevi*," Emily says. Her words are slurred, and her eyes are half-mast.

"I need him!" I yell. "Ask him to bring an EpiStick out here."

Leo's a sharp guy, so he disappears immediately. And thirty seconds later Wilson bounds into the room carrying an EpiStick. "What's a matter? Ooh! Got some hives there, honey. Damn. What's your allergy?" He uncaps the pen.

"She has no idea," I say, watching him.

"Wilson, do you have a spare?" Doc's voice asks from my phone. "Can't leave you without a dose."

"It's fine, Doc," the big center says with a smile. "I got two in my locker and a third somewhere in my equipment bag. And she needs it, Doc."

"Emily, are you okay with this?" I ask.

She nods fiercely. "Make it stop."

Wilson hands me the device, probably assuming that Emily and I actually know each other. "Just swing your arm, planting the tip against her thigh." He mimes the motion. "The needle will do its thing automatically."

Swing it? *Gulp*. That's not intimidating at all.

But Emily is watching me with frightened eyes, so there's really no choice. "Usually I get to know a girl before I grab her thigh, but..." With one hand, I push up Emily's skirt, revealing a few more inches of her black stockings. And then I plunk the EpiStick firmly against her thigh, just like Wilson said to do.

There's a loud, mechanical *click*, and Emily's eyes widen in shock.

"That's it," the big forward says encouragingly. "One banana...two bananas...three bananas..." After three seconds, Wilson reaches down and pulls the device away. He checks an indicator on the side. "Okay. You're dosed. It takes a minute or two. You might feel a little rush. But then it starts working pretty fast."

"And now you need to go to the emergency room," Doc's voice breaks in. "Everyone who self-doses should see a doctor afterward. They have to make sure there isn't a second wave to the reaction after the epinephrine wears off."

Emily leans back against the locker, her eyes closed. She puts a hand to her heart.

"Are you okay?"

"Yes," she whispers. "I'm just trying not to panic."

"Would you like some water?" I offer, straightening up.

To my surprise, she grabs my hand. "Don't go anywhere."

Okay, then. The lady gets what the lady wants. I sit down beside her again. "Do me a favor, though? Look at me, so I can tell if you're getting better or worse."

Her beautiful eyes blink open. They're a deep brown color, and they're focused on me. "Better, I think." She takes a deep breath. "My throat doesn't feel so thick anymore. The sensation is so strange, though. Like I can feel the drug moving through my bloodstream."

"Isn't it trippy?" Wilson agrees cheerfully.

"You *sound* better," Doc says. "Kids, get to the ER, okay?"

"Will do," I promise Doc.

"Who's gonna finish loading all this gear, though?" a female voice calls out.

I look up and see Heidi Jo, the GM's assistant, smirking at me. "Well, Dirk and…" I'm not sure who I can ask to bail me out.

"Just kidding, Jimbo. Who's a gullible boy? Dirk and I are already mostly done." Heidi Jo skips off toward the loading dock, a giant hockey bag on her shoulder. And Dirk—the new guy—follows her with two more bags. He just started with us this month, and he still looks a little overwhelmed by the chaos of game night.

Wilson rests a hand on my arm. "She looks better already. Her lips aren't as swollen."

I turn back to Emily and see that he's right. "That stuff is miraculous."

"Nice goal tonight," Emily says, blinking up at Wilson. "This is very surreal. Maybe I'm dreaming it."

Wilson laughs. "Drop by anytime. But I better refill my prescription first. Give this to the ER doc, okay?" Whistling, he hands over the empty EpiStick and then heads back toward the dressing room.

"Where's the nearest ER? Methodist, right?" I ask as I wake up my phone one-handed. Emily is still clutching my other hand. I'm trying not to notice how smooth her fingers feel against my skin.

"Methodist," Emily agrees with a sigh. "I don't want to go there."

"I'll bet. But Doc said you had to. And I promised." I stand up. "Come on. Your driver is waiting."

"Uber will be pricey. You have to let me pay you back."

"It's not an Uber," I say. "I'm your driver in this situation. The van smells like hockey gear, but there's no charge."

She huffs out a laugh. "Are you sure you don't mind?"

"Of course I'm sure." If I was having an odd and terrifying health problem, I'd want someone to drive me to the ER.

Tonight, Emily's someone is me.

"Right this way, Emily." I tug on her hand, and she stands, looking a little wobbly. "All right." I put an arm around her waist, which would seem really forward at any other moment.

She leans against me as we navigate back up the ramp and out the loading dock. I help her into the van's front seat, and I crank down the window. "Sit tight for a few minutes while I get the last of the stuff. Yell if you don't feel well."

"Honestly, I feel a lot better," she says. "Take your time."

I jog back inside and do a last sweep for any equipment that's been left behind. Then Dirk and I carry the last of it outside and toss it into the van.

He slams the back door. "All done here. Want me to park it at the Navy Yards?"

"I'll park it at home tonight," I say. "Meet you at the air terminal tomorrow."

"Sure," he grunts. "'Night, Jimbo."

"'Night. And thank you!"

But he's already gone.

By the time I ease the van onto 6th Avenue, it's midnight. Stadium traffic has cleared up, so the drive to the hospital only takes ten minutes. And I get lucky with an on-street parking space.

"How can you parallel park this thing?" Emily asks, watching me lean on the wheel.

"I'm a Brooklyn boy. I could parallel park the Staten Island Ferry on a postage stamp."

She laughs, which is how I know she's really on the mend.

I hop out of the van.

"You don't have to go with me," she says. "I've taken up enough of your time."

"Sorry." I shrug, locking the vehicle. "I can't just leave a woman alone in front of a hospital at midnight. What if they tell you to go somewhere else?"

She gives me a funny smile and doesn't press the issue.

When we reach the check-in desk, a militant-looking guy in a buzz-cut and scrubs gives Emily a long form to fill out.

"Seriously, you don't have to wait," she says, taking a seat to fill out the paperwork.

"I'm not leaving you here until I'm sure we're in the right place," I tell her.

"Then I don't know what I did to deserve you," she says, leaning over to attack the form, which seems to require a hundred pieces of personal information.

When she's done, we approach the desk again. "What's your health concern?" Mr. Grumpy asks.

"I had some kind of violent allergic reaction," Emily explains. She goes on to tell him about her symptoms and how Doc gave the go-ahead to apply Wilson's EpiStick. She lifts her sleeve to show him her hives, but the red spots have faded to nearly nothing.

"And you think it's okay to go around stabbing yourself with a stranger's medicine?" the man behind the desk barks.

"Not usually," Emily says, straightening her spine. "But this was an emergency and the doctor said he thought it was merited."

I practically have to wire my jaw shut to avoid jumping into their conversation, because this guy is being a first-class asshole. But I won't be that guy who talks over a woman who can speak for herself.

And I'm not the only one who's irritated, either. There's a slight young man standing ten or so feet behind him, holding a pen and a medical chart. He's simultaneously eavesdropping and making notes on someone else's clipboard chart.

"Fine," Mr. Militant says eventually. "Come on back. The standard procedure is three hours of observation following a dose of epinephrine."

"How much will it cost?" Emily asks. "I have a really high deductible."

"Not my department," he barks. "Now come on through before I give someone else your spot. And just you. No boyfriends."

Emily turns to me, wide-eyed. "Okay. Wow. Thank you for all you've done."

"It's nothing—"

"Let's go!" bellows the asshole, and Emily flinches.

"Go ahead," I say gently. "It's probably quieter back there." I give her a wink.

"Bye," she whispers, and then steps through the open gate, which clicks shut behind her.

The ass behind the desk flips the clipboard to the other man, whose name tag reads *Dr. Agarwal.* He catches it one handed. Then he gives Emily a quiet smile and beckons her toward the corridor beyond. So at least one person who works here isn't going to try to intimidate her.

Emily turns around one last time and waves at me. "Bye," she mouths. "Thank you."

I wave back. She disappears, and I realize too late that I didn't even get her phone number.

CHAPTER THREE

DID YOU GET ANY AUTOGRAPHS?

3

Emily

I feel so strange walking away from James. This has been one of the scariest nights of my life, and he was the only thing standing between me and a nervous breakdown.

Dr. Agarwal leads me to a bench in the hallway. "Sit here a second," he says. "I heard you describing your symptoms at the front desk. Would you describe the sensation in your throat as more of an itch or a burn?"

"Definitely an itch."

"And the person who gave you the shot of Epi is someone with a food allergy?"

"Yes. He took one look at me and told the doctor on the phone that it looked exactly like an allergic reaction."

"This friend—has he seen many allergic reactions? And this doctor was...?"

"Um..." I don't know how I'm going to explain this. "Are you a Brooklyn hockey fan?"

The doctor blinks. "Sort of? I watched them win the Cup."

"The rookie center—Wilson? He's the guy who gave me his EpiStick. I was outside the stadium at the loading dock when I started to feel so sick. And their equipment manager brought me in. They got the team doctor on the phone."

Dr. Agarwal laughs. "Well, that's a story you'll be telling for a while. Did you get any autographs?"

I shake my head. "Too busy freaking out."

"Okay. Do you have any idea what caused it?" Dr. Agarwal asks. "How much time passed between the last thing you ate and the onset of your symptoms?"

"Lots of time," I say. "We ate during the first period, and the hockey game was ending when I first felt my palms itch. And this has never happened to me before."

"What did you eat during the first period?"

"A barbecued brisket hoagie, fries, ketchup, a pickle. And a Coke. Regular, not diet."

"Alcohol?"

I shake my head. "It's a school night."

He taps his pen against his lip and then starts scribbling on his prescription pad. "First thing tomorrow morning, you call an allergist—here's two names. Make an appointment to be tested. We can't test you in the ER. You need to figure this out, okay? And you're going to fill this prescription for another EpiStick." He flips the page and writes some more. "These are pricey, but you need to carry it with you until you see the allergist."

"Okay? Sure. And what happens now?"

"Well..." He hesitates. "The protocol is for me to check your vitals and sit you down somewhere for three hours to make sure you don't experience any labored breathing or a return of your symptoms. But I'll make a deal with you."

"What's that?" God, I want to go home.

"I can tell from looking at you that the epinephrine worked. You're not in the midst of an allergic crisis. So, if you take a seat in the waiting room—or the cafeteria—for three hours, I'll come and check on you at…" He looks at his watch. "Three a.m. And if you're still doing well, I'll send you on your way. But you won't be logged as a patient. If you're still smiling in three hours, you can just tear this up." He takes my paperwork off the clipboard and hands it to me.

"Really? You can do that?"

"Yeah, I have a high deductible, too. But *please* don't leave the hospital. And don't eat anything. Only water to drink."

"No problem." I stand up.

"Don't go home, okay? Otherwise, I'll spend my break looking for you, and that's just mean."

"I promise!" I laugh. "I'll be on one of those ugly chairs outside."

"Good. Go. The secret exit is over there." He guides me toward a different door than the one I came in. "You're saving me paperwork, anyway. My gut says you'll be just fine. And if my gut is wrong—"

"—I'm only ten paces from the desk."

"Exactly. Where you'd ask for me by name. Meanwhile, I'm setting an alarm to come and find you." He taps his watch.

"Thank you! I really appreciate this." I'm walking backwards toward the door. Then I make my escape to the waiting room.

I scan the room. Only five minutes have passed, but James is nowhere to be seen.

Of course. It's after midnight, and he's gone home. I'd let him go before I'd said a proper goodbye. It was that grumpy triage nurse's fault. I'd let him intimidate me out of getting James's full name and contact information.

SARINA BOWEN

The guy deserves a thank you, at the very minimum. I'll have to figure out how to contact him tomorrow.

For a few minutes, I just stand around and get my bearings. There's really no rush to find a seat. I'm going to be here for hours. Besides, the doctor said I could have water, and that sounds good right about now. There must be a vending machine somewhere.

As I pace the edges of the room, I see the glow of a Coke machine from around the corner. And when I come closer, I notice a tall, strong-looking guy in a Brooklyn Bruisers jacket feeding a dollar bill into the machine.

"James!" I cry in surprise, and he whirls around.

Then the most beautiful smile breaks across his face. It's so wide that I wonder if it's even for me. "Hey, back so soon? Did you miss me?"

Would it be strange to admit that I did?

"L," I guess.

"Doh!" James says, giving the hangman a leg. I'm about to lose this game. I've got BRYAN but the last name is eluding me. It reads _ R _ _ _ _ E R.

"U," I try.

He shakes his head, and the hangman gets a bowtie.

"C?"

James gives the hangman a pair of glasses. He's trying not to let me lose.

"O?"

"Yeah!" He fills one in for the third letter. But I'm still stumped.

"Uncle," I whimper. "I guess my knowledge of NHL hall-of-famers isn't as great as I thought it was."

"But you got Lemieux!" he says, tapping our last game with his pen. "This guy is Bryan Trottier."

"Who?"

James chuckles. "He won six Stanley Cups as a player and one as an assistant coach. Here—it's your turn to hang me." He hands over the pen.

I set it down. "What if you just told me about your job, instead? How did you end up as the Bruisers' equipment manager?"

He shrugs, and his smile is so cute that I feel a little fluttery inside. That's how I know my allergic reaction is truly over—I care more about the company I'm keeping than I do about my health scare.

"I've always loved hockey," he tells me. "I used to play in a league at Chelsea Piers. Then I took a job there, because it got me a discount. So I was working at the rink—sharpening skates, driving the Zamboni…"

"You drive the Zamboni?" I squeak. There are probably hearts in my eyes right now.

"Not in Brooklyn," he says quickly. "I mean—only in emergencies at the practice rink. Mostly, I handle all the players' gear —I make sure their pads are clean and on the jet when we travel. I sharpen their skates however they like that done. I order the sticks and the tape." He shrugs again. "Honestly, I applied for this job on a whim the spring before I graduated from high school. Was stunned to get called in for an interview. Even more stunned to be hired. That was almost four years ago now."

"And now hockey is your livelihood! That is so amazing."

"My father is less amazed than you are," he says, tilting his handsome head back against the wall. "He says I'm wasting time on a job that has no future."

"Seriously?" I make a sound of outrage. "What exactly does he want you to *do* that's so damn important?"

He laughs uncomfortably. "Well, Dad's an electrician. He has his own business, and he wanted me to join him. Still does. Every time I see him, he asks me when I'm going to be ready to get my license."

I groan. "He and my mother should form a club. Hell— they've probably already had their membership cards made for the Tell Your Kid What To Do With His Life Club."

"You, too, huh?" He gives me a lopsided smile that is practically irresistible. "What does your mom want you to be when you grow up?"

"I'm studying education. She wants me to get a business degree, just like my boyfriend did."

He blinks. And maybe I'm tired enough to hallucinate, but I swear he looks a little bummed now. "Business," he says flatly.

"Yeah. She thinks I'll never pay off my student loans. But it's not going to be that bad. I get financial aid, and I live at home to keep costs down."

"You're braver than me. I moved out of my parents' house so I could stop listening to my dad complain about the future of his business without me. Also, I have three sisters, so..." He chuckles. "Was kind of looking forward to having my own bathroom anyway."

"Three! I always wanted sisters. Or a brother. It's been just my mom and me since I can remember."

"I have a huge family," James says. "Sometimes it's great, but sometimes it's a pain in the ass. I'm still surrounded by them, even if I don't live at home. So my dad still gets his kicks in."

"He's crazy. And I'm not just saying that because I'm a hockey nut."

He grins.

"Not everyone gets to spend every day immersed in something they really love. That's really special, and I'm sorry he can't see it."

"Thank you," he says softly. Our gazes are locked now, and his eyes are the color of melted chocolate. "I'm sorry, too. The way he built up his business is pretty impressive, you know? It's just not what I want to do all day."

"Then you shouldn't," I insist. "What's it like traveling with the team?"

His grin widens. "It's like summer camp with really good food. I've been to some great restaurants and some really nice hotels. I've watched over three hundred games standing two feet from the ice in every major league hockey stadium in North America. With the guys, I've gone skating on the river in Ottawa, and swimming in the Pacific Ocean."

"Yeah, you really ought to quit that job," I say with a smile.

"I know, right?"

"Can you tell me some gossip about the team?" I bat my eyelashes at him.

"No, ma'am." He's still smiling, but he shakes his head. "I don't talk about them, because it wouldn't be right."

"I know! I was kidding." I reach over and squeeze his arm. And, wow, it's like squeezing iron. "Seriously. I wouldn't want you to."

"I mean, it's tempting to tell you which player eats the same strawberry jam and peanut butter sandwich before every game. And which one still carries around his lucky jockstrap from high school..."

"Omigod!" I yelp. "Now I'm dying of curiosity. But not about the sandwich thing—I read that on Puck Rakers. It's Castro."

Now James cracks up. "Really? That's out in the world?"

"Yup. Someone must have ratted him out."

"Well, it wasn't me."

"Of course it wasn't you. We've already established that." That's when my phone rings. I actually startle, because it's late, and I've forgotten that anyone else in the world exists besides me and James.

When I check the phone, it's Charles calling. Oh boy. "Hello?" I answer, looking around to see if anyone will give me a dirty look for talking on my cell. But the waiting room crowd has really thinned out.

"Emily! You didn't answer my texts. I wanted to make sure you were okay."

"Charles, it's really late, so I didn't expect your messages. Actually, I'm in the waiting room at the ER at Methodist."

"*What?*"

He freaks out a little, and I hurry to explain everything that happened. "I'm fine now. I swear."

"God, I had no idea. Do you need me to come and get you?"

I *almost* say yes just out of spite. He hadn't listened when I'd told him I wasn't feeling well. He'd been too busy pleasing his clients.

But I don't really want Charles to rush over here. He's already home, and I don't need help anymore. "Go to sleep. It's late. I'll Uber home."

He argues halfheartedly before agreeing to stay home.

"Goodnight, honey. Call me tomorrow to let me know how you are."

"Sure. 'Night."

"Love you."

I end the call so I don't have to say it back.

"Is that the boyfriend?" James asks.

"That was the boyfriend," I say with a sigh. "He probably feels guilty for blowing me off when I said I felt sick."

"Come again?" James's voice is barely above a whisper. When I turn to him, his whole body has gone strangely still. "Did you say he blew you off? Was he at the *game?*"

"Well, yeah. He and some clients. They were headed into Manhattan for drinks, and I bailed because I felt off. He was irritated."

"Irritated," James says slowly. "Because his girlfriend was having a *life-threatening allergic reaction?*"

"He didn't know that," I say softly. "Neither did I. We both just assumed it was nothing."

"Okay," James says carefully. "But if I was seeing somebody, and she felt off, I'd want to know about it. She wouldn't be able to shake me. Just saying. My ass would be parked in the emergency room makin' sure she was okay."

"I bet it would," I admit. His ass is currently parked next to mine, and we don't even know each other. "She'd be a lucky girl."

Our eyes meet, and I feel my face heat from embarrassment. Did that sound flirty? I think it did. And now we're having a staring contest.

Luckily, it's interrupted. "Emily?" Dr. Agarwal says. "Looks like you're still feeling all right. So I guess you can finally go home."

CHAPTER FOUR

WORST. TRIP. EVER.

4

Emily

"A *tick* bite?" It's the last thing I expected the allergist to ask me. "Why?"

"Because I'm working on a theory," he says, crossing his arms across his lab coat. "Have you been bitten within the last few months?"

"Well, yes," I admit. "One time. I was bitten by a tick on the world's most stressful golf trip."

The doctor blinks. "Why was it stressful? Because of the ticks?"

"No, because I'm terrible at golf, and my boyfriend was trying to impress his boss." I know I'm oversharing now, but I've been in this doctor's office for over two hours already, and I'm starting to lose it. First, I endured a battery of prick tests which made my back itch, then I had a blood test, and now I just want to go home.

"When and where did you receive this bite?"

SARINA BOWEN

"Um, November. It was right after Halloween, and we were at a resort in North Carolina."

It was the only one of Charles's corporate boondoggles that had involved travel. I'd hated everything about it except for the hotel room with the king-sized bed in it. The moment Charles removed my dress, though, he'd found the tick. After that, we were both too squicked out for sexy times.

Worst. Trip. Ever.

"But what does a tick bite have to do with an allergic reaction?" I ask. "Do you think I have Lyme disease?"

"No, but I'm pretty sure you have a different tick-borne illness called alpha-gal syndrome. It's carried by the Lone Star tick, which lives in warmer climates like North Carolina. It can transmit a particular sugar molecule into the blood stream. And in some people, this triggers a delayed allergic response to red meat."

"Red meat," I say slowly. "All of it?"

"All of it," he says firmly.

And I just gulp.

Two days later, I'm sitting at the NYU library, wondering what to eat for dinner.

I'm still trying to get my head around everything the doctor told me. Before I left his office, he gave me a sheaf of papers to read and another prescription for an epinephrine auto-injector.

Honestly it hasn't even sunk in yet. I'm not used to thinking so hard about what I can and cannot eat.

My mother doesn't understand it at all, either. She thinks

I'm exaggerating. "It's not pork, just pork broth," she said last night when I turned down her homemade soup.

"I can't eat that," I'd protested. "It could make me sick."

She'd rolled her eyes at me. And part of me doesn't blame her. Because the whole thing sounds crazy. A food allergy you can catch from a bug? It sounds like a sci-fi plot.

My new EpiStick is tucked into a special pocket in my book bag. If I order take-out food that is somehow cross contaminated with red meat, I won't die. Probably.

"You have to be really careful for a while," the doctor had warned me. "Some people recover from alpha-gal after a year or two and can eat whatever they want. But do your body a favor and avoid the allergens for a nice long time. It's impossible to guess the magnitude of your next allergic response. Read the labels, ask questions, and keep your EpiStick nearby."

Right. No problem.

When I can't stand my gurgling stomach any longer, I head for the cafeteria and order a Caesar salad. And I buy a small bag of peanuts, because I need the protein, but I'm afraid to eat any meat at all.

Chicken and fish are supposed to be no trouble for me. The problem is that I can't quite forget the feeling of my swelled-up throat and itching lips.

Just as I carry my strange meal to a table, my phone rings. It's Charles. I fumble to set the tray down and answer it quickly. "Hi, baby," I say quietly. "How are you?"

"Fine," he says, sounding a little testy. "Are you sure you can't come out tonight? There's still forty minutes until our reservation."

"There's no way," I say immediately. "Big test tomorrow."

Besides, he's entertaining clients at a steak place, which is the *last* place I want to go right now. I brought this up when he first asked if I was free tonight, and he'd said, "They have other food, too. You can order the fish."

But I'm too freaked out by the whole thing to walk into a steak restaurant just yet. I'd have to quiz the staff about whether the foods are grilled together in the same spot. And I don't want to learn that new skill under Charles's critical eye.

"You could have dinner and then leave before drinks," he wheedles. "I miss you."

I'm sure he misses me. But I'm also sure that he hates the idea of showing up single if his clients are bringing dates. "Sorry," I say for at least the third time. "We'll see each other this weekend."

"Yeah. Okay," he mumbles. This weekend isn't as important to him. He doesn't care as much about catching up on *The Crown* with me and sleeping late on Sundays the way we used to. These days it's all about the job.

"Have a nice dinner," I tell him, because I need to get off the phone. "I'll call you tomorrow."

"Fine. Love you," he says, but it sounds grudging.

"Love you, too," I say before we hang up.

A few minutes later, I find myself staring at my salad, thinking about the first time Charles ever said he loved me. We'd been in tenth grade, and I'd been dazzled. I'd felt like I'd found a winning lottery ticket.

Lately, though? I can't remember the last time that Charles and I had a great time together, just the two of us. He's so detached, and I feel myself accepting it as the new normal.

This is just your anxiety talking, I remind myself. A girl shouldn't get too introspective the night before a test.

So I put in another two hours' worth of work. When I'm done, I look through my phone for James's email address. I'd promised him I'd let him know what the doctor said. I open an email window and start typing.

Dear James,

Thank you again for everything you did for me last Saturday night. I have never needed a stranger's help like that before. And instead of letting me be lonely and afraid at the ER, you actually made my time in that waiting room fun.

So thank you for saving the day.

I promised to tell you what I'd learned, so I hope you like science fiction. The allergist says that I have alpha-gal syndrome. That means that I became allergic to red meat after a tick bite. You're probably rolling your eyes right now but it's actually a real thing. I had to Google it, too.

So I'll be fine, but I won't be enjoying another barbecue brisket sandwich at the hockey stadium. And I guess that's just as well because those tickets were expensive and that sandwich was twenty bucks.

You've already done so much, but can I ask for one more favor? Can you tell me which pharmacy is closest to where you guys practice in Brooklyn? I would like to buy Wilson a gift card. It turns out that EpiSticks cost a small fortune. I can't buy him a new one, because you need a prescription. But I could buy the gift card and include a thank-you note.

Finally, I'd like to thank you as well. Could I buy you a non-meat pizza some night when you're in town?

Thanks again,

Emily

. . .

After I write the email, I reread my work. And then I have the urge to hit Delete. I didn't know that I was going to invite him out for pizza until I wrote that. But it seemed wrong to thank Wilson and not James.

Although it also seems a little wrong to ask a guy other than Charles out to dinner. But it's just a friendly pizza, right? It doesn't mean I have a crush on him. Or that I feel the pull to see him again.

After staring at it for a couple more minutes, I finally just hit Send. He probably won't even reply.

I'm crossing the East River on the subway when an answer pops into my inbox.

My finger hovers over the new message. If he turns down dinner, I'll be mortified.

And why is that, exactly? Why do I even care? It's not like I have lots of time and extra cash to spend on cute boys who work with the greatest hockey team in the world.

I hold my breath and open the message.

CHAPTER FIVE

FULL
BODIED

5

James

On an evening in early December, I'm loading hockey pads into bags when the team comes through the dressing room after a video session.

"Who wants to grab dinner?" Silas asks his teammates.

"Your girl is out of town?" Castro guesses.

"Of course his girl is out of town," Crikey says. "Any guy willing to dine with me the night before a road trip is single or temporarily single."

"Maybe I just like your scruffy face," Silas says, giving him a cheesy wink. "Do you put out on the first date?"

"Only if you buy me dinner first. What are we eating?"

"I'm in the mood for pizza," Silas says.

And that's when I start to panic. I'm meeting Emily at Grimaldi's in forty minutes. And I do *not* need the entire hockey team tagging along.

"Pizza sounds good," Crikey agrees. "Who else is coming?"

Bayer, Drake, and Tankiewicz all raise their hands.

"I'm in," Castro says. "Heidi is having dinner with her father tonight."

"He still hates you?" I hear myself ask. Heidi Jo's dad is the league commissioner, and he did not want his baby girl to date a hockey player.

"He's over it. You coming out for pizza, Jimbo?"

"Um..." I have to think fast. "Did you guys see there's a new noodle shop on Court?

"Any good?" Castro asks.

"I haven't tried it, but the menu looks great."

"But it's my turn to pick," Silas argues. "And I want pizza."

"Weren't you at Grimaldi's, like, two nights ago?" I try.

"What, like that's weird?" Silas scoffs. "Why the sudden hostility toward the best pizza in Brooklyn?"

"No reason," I mumble. But I sure hope they end up going somewhere else.

No such luck. When I walk through Grimaldi's door a half hour later, I spot six hockey players together at a big table. I almost manage to sneak past them, but the waitress—Nancy Elizabeth—looks up and smiles. "Jimbo! Should I grab another chair?"

"Uh, nope. A friend asked me to meet her here."

"A *friend*." Castro's eyes light up. "What kind of friend? Are you on a date, Jimbo?"

"No way," I say quickly. Not that I don't wish I was. "Like I said, a *friend*."

"But you combed your hair." Silas is grinning now.

"People do that," I grumble.

"Guys, who thinks Jimbo's hair looks extra good tonight?" Castro asks.

Six hockey players raise their hands.

"Later guys," I say, hurrying away from their table.

I swear someone says, "Oh, this could be fun," as I walk away.

Luckily, Emily is waiting for me at a table against the back wall, far away from the Bruisers. And, wow, my memory didn't lie. She's super pretty, with flashing dark eyes and a quick smile.

"Hey there," I say, leaning down to give her a friendly peck on the cheek. I'm Italian. We do that. Although maybe it was a mistake, because she smells like flowers, and my body tightens at the nearness of her. I step back and take in her clear skin and healthy glow. "You look great."

"James," she says with a smile. "Are you implying that I didn't look great at three a.m. after breaking out in full-body hives?"

"Nobody implied that," I say with a chuckle. "It's just that not-on-death's-doorstep is also a good look on you." I pull out my chair and have a seat. Out of my peripheral vision, I see a hockey player stand up to peek in my direction. At least they're too far away to throw things at me. "Should we start with a cocktail? I ask. "Sounds like you've had quite the week."

"Of course. Do you need the drink menu?" She passes it to me.

"Nope, I'm good," I say as Nancy Elizabeth approaches.

"Hi kids, can I get you two a cocktail to start?"

"What's good?" Emily asks, scanning the wine list.

"I'm always in the mood for prosecco," Nancy Elizabeth says. "But if you're looking for a red, I like the chianti. It's full bodied without being too tannic. And if you're looking for a great date, I recommend Jimbo. He's also full bodied, has nice manners, and is a great tipper."

Emily blinks in confusion.

But I know exactly what's happening, and I just want to sink down into the floor. "Nancy Elizabeth," I say stiffly. "Whatever they're paying you to prank me, I'll double it if you stop."

"What fun would that be?" she asks with a sniff.

"I'll have the chianti," Emily says. "Thanks for the recommendation."

"And I'll have the—"

"Oh, I know what to bring you," the waitress mutters. "You always get the same thing."

"You don't know that!" I call as she starts to walk away. "I just might surprise you."

Emily follows the waitress with her intelligent, dark eyes. "You come here a lot?"

"Too much, apparently. And so do those chuckleheads." I jerk my thumb in the direction of the players. Just as Emily turns to look, they all drop into their seats again, like prairie dogs avoiding a coyote.

Fuckers.

"So how was your week?" I ask, trying to change the subject.

"Dreadful," she says with a little smile. "It's not every week you learn that a tick gave you an allergy. But what about you? Were you dead on your feet the next day?"

I totally was. "Oh, it was fine," I lie. "We slept on the jet."

And it's true—I did sleep. I slept so well that when I woke up, I was duct-taped to my seat, which is a favorite Bruisers prank. But I leave that detail out.

I got even the next night, anyway. After the game, Castro, Trevi, and Baby Bayer emerged from the shower to find only hot-pink briefs in their lockers. I'd been saving those up for a special occasion.

And—this made my revenge even sweeter—a reporter who was in the locker room for interviews made a crack about them. Leo Trevi is pretty quick on his feet, so he said they were wearing them for breast cancer awareness.

But I still feel like I got the edge on them. It's not even Breast Cancer Awareness month.

Emily is eyeing the menu. "This is going to sound ridiculous, but this week I've been terrified to eat—even things that I know don't have red meat in them. I keep thinking about how my throat started itching, and it's turned me off of food."

"Oh, hell. I'm sorry. Are you getting enough to eat?"

"I'll be fine. But if it's okay with you, I'd prefer not to get meat on the pizza. Or we could get separate ones."

"Who needs meat? The white pizza with garlic is amazing. Let's get a salad with chicken on it, too, so that you can get some protein."

Her expression softens. "Thank you. That sounds amazing."

"A glass of chianti for the lady." We both look up to see that our drinks have arrived. That shouldn't be surprising, except it isn't Nancy Elizabeth who's brought them. Instead, it's Castro, wearing the waitress's nametag and apron over his jeans and Brooklyn T-shirt.

"Omigod," Emily breathes. Her eyes sort of glaze over. It's not an allergic reaction this time. She's starstruck.

This is why I will never have a girlfriend. This right here.

"Dude, are you moonlighting?" I grumble at Castro. "That seven-figure salary isn't cutting it for you?"

"I just like to help out," he says in a smarmy voice. "And it didn't seem like you were going to introduce us to your new friend. Hi." He sets Emily's wine glass down on the table and then offers his hand. "I'm Jason Castro. I just want you to know that Jimbo is a really stand-up guy. He's a really attentive friend. Except for tonight, that is. He's prompt, he has good personal hygiene, and he volunteers for the Boys and Girls Club of Brooklyn."

I take my beer out of his hand. Then I reach out an arm and physically push him away from the table. "Thanks for stopping by."

There's a chorus of snickers from the front of the restaurant.

I want to die. Even if this isn't really a date, Emily is the most beautiful girl I've almost shared a pizza with. And it would be nice if I could finish a conversation with her. Just once. Is it really too much to ask?

"Have you decided what you want for dinner?" Castro pulls Nancy Elizabeth's order pad out of his pocket and clicks the button on her pen.

"Yes. I'd like fifteen minutes of peace and a new job."

Emily lets out a shriek of laughter.

"Such *hostility* from table thirty-three," Castro complains. "Are you ordering food or not?"

"Yeah, but send Nancy Elizabeth over here, please. Emily has a food allergy, and she'd really prefer to explain it to someone who actually knows the menu."

"Oh." Jason flinches. "Good idea. I'll send her over. You kids have fun."

Nancy Elizabeth returns to take our order—and to assure Emily that red meat will not *touch* our order. "I will make that salad myself," she promises. "And I'll watch them make your pizza."

"Thank you," Emily says with obvious relief, and I make a mental note to tip Nancy Elizabeth well tonight.

"Also?" I say as I hand back my menu. "Keep those yokels away from me."

"That might be more difficult than getting your order right," she says.

"Try," I insist, and she just smiles.

I forget all about the Bruisers for a little while, thankfully. Emily is easy company. But then Drake delivers the appetizers, and Silas delivers the pizza.

"There are a lot of people named Nancy Elizabeth who work in this restaurant," Emily says as Silas plunks a steaming-hot pizza in front of us.

"And they are all so masculine," I add.

Silas puffs out his chest. "Thank you for noticing. Can I get anyone another drink?"

"Would it make you go away if I said no?" I ask.

"Probably not."

"Then you'd better bring more alcohol."

When he walks away, I let out a sigh. "I'm sorry. I should have picked a different restaurant."

Emily plucks a piece of hot pizza off the tray and puts it on her plate. "I don't know, James. The fact that they keep coming over here says something about you."

"Does it say: James has really immature friends?"

She shakes her head and smiles. "It says that your friends think highly of you. We only tease the people we love."

"That is a really nice way of looking at it."

Her smile warms me from across the table. She takes a bite

of pizza, and then she *moans*. Not just a little moan, either. But a lush, orgasmic noise that makes my body tighten with expectation. "Omigod this is *heaven*. I've been *soooo* hungry."

Me too, beautiful. And I'm not talking about the food.

"And I'm not even afraid to eat this, because Nancy Elizabeth promised me I could."

Aw, man. Suddenly, I want to bring her every meatless dish in Brooklyn, and then watch her eat it. I brace myself for another moan as another bite of pizza disappears in Emily's lovely mouth. And, yup. There it is.

"Sorry," she says with a giggle. "I'm usually a very polite eater."

"Don't you dare be sorry. Swear to God, politeness can be overrated." That statement was brought to you by my dick, which is not feeling so polite right now. Maybe I have some kind of pizza-based food kink, because Emily is making this into a sexual experience for me.

Her eyes fly to mine, and we stare at each other for a long beat. So maybe I'm not the only one who's having a really good time right now.

If only she'd ditch her boyfriend, we could spend weekends in my bed. Naked. Making love and eating pizza.

Down, boy. This is a casual, friendly dinner. At least it's supposed to be.

But let's be honest. I like Emily. A lot. And I intend to let her know that as soon as I can.

CHAPTER SIX

OOPS I SLIPPED

6

Emily

I don't know how this happened. But I'm having more fun with James over a pizza than I have had in a *long* time. I'll admit that I started off the evening a little starstruck. Having the attention of a table full of famous athletes is pretty crazy.

But after a while, I sort of forget who they are on the ice. The more they needle James, the more I come to see them like a big, rowdy family of brothers. And "Jimbo" is the baby brother in this scenario—the one they tease and torture but love to death.

And I can see why. James is such a great guy. He tells me stories about his other big family—the Italian grandmas and aunts and his three younger siblings.

"Your house must have been crowded growing up," I point out. "Maybe that's why a locker room full of overgrown boys doesn't bother you that much."

His dark eyes widen. "I have had that same thought *many* times. My job doesn't require a great deal of skill. But I'm really good at tuning out drama and focusing on the task at hand."

"That is a special skill, though." I point out. I have the feeling that James underestimates himself. I'd hate it if his father convinced him that his job doesn't matter.

The players probably worship him. And I don't think anyone has ever listened to me as carefully as he's doing right now.

Someone approaches our table. I look up to see that it's Silas—the goalie. "All done here?" he asks, clearing away our empty dishes and balancing the pizza pan on his forearm like a pro. "Can I get you anything else? Coffee? Another glass of wine? Jimbo's high school yearbook photo? Believe it or not, he used to use even more product in his hair. This is actually an improvement. We're working on it."

James just rolls his eyes.

"Dessert?" Silas asks.

"Sure," I chirp. After all, I intended to treat James to a special meal. "What's good here?"

"I'll send you the chef's special," Silas says with a wink.

"What's the chef's special?" I ask after he walks away.

"This is the first I've heard of it, and I'm kind of afraid to find out," James says with a sigh.

"Your friends are fun, I'm having a really good time tonight," I say quietly. "It's refreshing to spend some time with people who don't always take life so seriously."

James's eyes warm. "I'm glad. You deserve to have some fun after the stressful week you just had."

"Right," I agree. But it's just dawning on me that my strange new diagnosis isn't the only stressful thing in my life. Everything is such a grind lately. Even the parts that are supposed to be fun—like going out with Charles—have turned into a chore.

How did that happen, exactly? And how can I make it stop?

This thought is interrupted by the appearance of a restaurant staffer. He's carrying a plate—no, a *platter*—filled with dessert items. There are tiny little fruit tarts and miniature Italian cookies and, in the center, a chocolate lava cake.

But, unfortunately, there is a giant burning sparkler in the center of it, shaped like a heart, and lighting up the restaurant like a beacon. Everyone in the crowded restaurant turns to stare.

"One Amore Special for table thirty-three," the waiter says, sliding the platter onto the table. "Enjoy."

Just then, *"That's Amore"* starts playing loudly over the sound system. The entire restaurant cheers.

James closes his eyes and sighs. And I crack up.

We eat the lava cake in its entirety. He's in a better mood now that all the hockey players have finally left. They also paid our bill, though, which means that I didn't even manage to treat dinner like I'd planned.

"Oh, please," James argues. "You paid just by putting up with that. Besides, if you want to treat me again sometime, I'm available." He sets down his dessert fork and gives me flirty eyes. "Anytime. But only at an undisclosed and distant location."

"How distant?" I ask, smiling like a lunatic. The idea of another dinner with James makes me happier than it should. Considering we're just friends.

"I hear Fiji has good restaurants."

We laugh together, and our gazes hold a little longer than is polite. I'm flirting with him. And I shouldn't be doing that.

Rein it in, Emily. Get a grip on yourself. "I should go," I say suddenly. "I have some studying to do."

"Of course." He puts his napkin on the table and stands. "Let me take you home."

"You don't have to," I hedge.

"It's really no problem at all. We're probably heading for the same train station." He holds out a hand to help me up.

Swoon!

I put my hand in his for no particular reason and let him lead me out of the restaurant.

Outside, James makes a groan of irritation. And when I look up, there's a man in a suit standing on the sidewalk holding a small white sign—the way drivers do at the airport. In marker, it reads: "Jimbo (a GREAT guy) and Emily."

Behind him waits a bright orange stretch limo.

I let out a shriek of laughter. "They just won't quit, will they?"

"Apparently not," he mutters. Then he steps up to the limo's back door and opens it. "So let's head home in comfort." He holds the door open for me like a true gentleman.

Still laughing, I skip over and climb in.

Somehow, we both grow quiet on the ride to Bensonhurst. I spend much of the time trying not to stare at James, who's seated on the leather seat opposite mine. There's something intimate about the dark quiet of the luxury vehicle as it glides past the lights of Brooklyn.

I become overly conscious of James, who's a bigger man than Charles. His limbs are long, his jaw is square, and his shoulders are so broad that I imagine I could rest my head on one of them with room to spare.

Stop it, I coach myself. *We are not going to recline on James's big, solid body.*

He watches me, too. And he gives me a slow, private smile, as if he can read my thoughts.

It doesn't matter, though. The car pulls up outside my building, and our time together is over.

James thanks the driver and tells him not to wait. "I can get home on my own from here," he says. Then he gets out and walks me up to the entrance to the small apartment building where I've lived most of my life.

I wonder what sort of building James lives in.

Then I kick myself for wondering.

I turn around to say goodbye, and we're face to face, gazes locked.

He gives me a slow, sexy smile, but doesn't say anything.

"I can't invite you in," I blurt out. "I have a boyfriend."

His grin widens. "I remember. But, see, he's the wrong guy for you."

"How do you know?" I squeak.

"Because the right guy is me," he says simply.

Swoon!

"But it's okay if you're not on board yet," he adds. "We'll talk another time. Can I just have a friendly hug good night?"

"Sure," I say, my mind racing. The conversation has taken a strange turn, and I definitely haven't processed everything he just said. My poor little muddled brain is stuck on *the right guy is me*.

Nobody has ever said something so sexy to me before. Never ever.

Now James is opening his arms wide, waiting patiently. So it's up to me to step forward.

I do, because who could resist?

When I lean in, a pair of strong arms closes around me, and I bump up against a very hard chest. *Yowza.* And then? James leans down, brushing his face against mine, like a friendly cat. And when I turn my chin in surprise, a pair of surprisingly soft lips kiss mine.

It's quick, I suppose. Just a brush and a brief press. But it still makes me shiver and gasp.

"Oops, I slipped," he says, not sounding sorry at all. Then he drops his arms and steps back, leaving me shellshocked for a moment.

I just stand there like an idiot, trying to process that lovely little kiss.

"Goodnight, Emily," he says softly. "Be well. Thank you for inviting me out to dinner."

"Y-you're welcome," I stammer, blinking.

He tries the front door of my building, but it's locked. "Do you have your keys?" He smiles at me.

"Yes," I say, finally coming unstuck. I plunge my hand into my pocket and fish them out. He waits politely while I unlock the door. "Goodnight," I say, just before walking in.

"'Night, sweetheart."

I give him one last wave and a sheepish smile. Then I make myself go inside.

The next evening, when I come home from a long day of work and school, there's an envelope waiting for me on the kitchen table. The envelope is Bruisers purple.

When I open it, there's a ticket envelope inside, and two seats for a game next week. There's a message scrawled on the envelope in black ink: *For you and Mr. Wrong. —J.*

Oh boy. Charles would hate that.

The tickets are in Row D, and they have a face value of $130. *Each.* But at least I have the comfort of knowing James probably didn't have to pay for them.

I reread the note twice, and then tuck the tickets into my wallet and recycle the note.

He *knows* I have a boyfriend, but he gave me two tickets anyway.

So what choice do I have? I pull out my phone and invite Charles to go with me.

It's just that I have no idea whether he'll say yes.

CHAPTER SEVEN

ARE YOU SOMEONE IMPORTANT?

Emily

I'm waiting outside the Brooklyn stadium for Charles.

He's late. This is not particularly unusual. He literally will not leave his office until every one of his superiors is gone. And if they ask him for one last task? "I always say yes," he tells me. "Always. That's how you get ahead. There are five other guys in my program, and I am making every one of them look like a slacker."

This is why I'm standing outside on a frigid winter night, alone, watching the subway exit for Charles's well-dressed form.

I get it. I really do. I admire Charles so much. I always have.

But lately his job is just a drag. Because I know how Charles operates. And five years from now it will be exactly like this. He'll be working his way up the food chain. He'll have first-year associates that report to him, but that won't matter. There will still be people to impress and new reasons to stay late at work.

Is it selfish to wonder why it's never my turn? I would like —just once—to be the person he dropped everything for.

If I bring it up, I know exactly what he'll say. *I've only had this job for six months, Emily. I'm on probation.* And he would be right, and I'd be the whiner in this scenario.

This whiner's toes are very cold, though. And through the glass walls of the stadium, I can see all the happy fans moving slowly up the escalators toward their seats.

I pull out my phone and text him. ***It's cold, so I'm going to wait for you inside the lobby. It's mayhem in there, but you can text me when you come out of the subway, and I'll find you.***

My phone rings a moment later, just as I'm joining the line to have my bag inspected. It's Charles. So I step out of the damn line again and take the call. "Hello?"

"Honey, where are you?"

"At the hockey game, remember?" Oh my God, he *doesn't* remember. "You can still make it."

"No, I'm sorry. But I can't blow off this other thing."

My heart drops. "What other thing? If you're running late, I can probably leave your ticket at Will Call."

"We can't go to the hockey game tonight. I'm sorry. And I still need you to come to this art opening with me in SoHo."

"An art opening," I echo. Has the man lost his mind? "We have seats in row D!"

"Honey, we just *went* to a hockey game. And my client's daughter is part of a group exhibition at a gallery tonight. It will be fun. I changed our calendar yesterday. Didn't you see it?"

My heart thumps, and I can actually feel hot, liquid anger

pumping through my veins along with my blood. "No, Charles. I didn't see it. But if you were going to bail, you should have had the decency to say so in person, so I could have invited someone else."

"Who?"

"I don't *know*," I say through clenched teeth. "But I guess it doesn't matter now, does it?"

"It doesn't matter if you don't use the tickets," he says. "That guy won't know, Emily. And it's just a hockey game."

"I *like* hockey," I yelp. "And I'm *not* going to an art opening."

"It was on the calendar!"

"*Your* calendar," I shriek. "I'm not your secretary. It's not my job to look at the calendar every fifteen minutes to see if you've shifted something."

He sighs like I've disappointed him. "Emily, we're both so busy. I need you to be the kind of girlfriend who shares a calendar. We lead busy lives."

I need you to be... I'm so tired of those words.

"But maybe I'm just not that person," I say curtly. "Maybe you need to be the kind of boyfriend who doesn't run our relationship like it's another one of your spreadsheets."

That's my anger talking. But I feel like being his girlfriend is a role I've been auditioning for since middle school. "He's going to be a great man, Emily," my mother often says. "He might run the world someday."

Right this second, I can't even remember why that ever seemed important. I don't want to run the world. I just want to watch some hockey.

"You're angry," says Captain Obvious.

"Yes, I am," I admit.

"Then maybe we should take a break," he says.

My mouth falls open. *Oh my God.* Charles is breaking up with me? Over a calendar miscommunication?

"We'll talk tonight, when we're calmer," he says.

I exhale. Of course he's not breaking up with me. "Okay, we'll do that. I'm going to this hockey game."

"So you've said. Call me before you go to bed."

"Okay," I clip. "Goodbye."

He disconnects.

I rejoin the security line. There's still an hour before the puck drops, because I wanted to get here in time to scout out a meatless meal and to watch warmups.

But that also means the organization might be able to use this extra ticket. So once I'm inside, I find the customer-service window, and I hand it over to the woman behind the desk. "James—the equipment tech—gifted me two tickets. But I only need one."

A blonde woman standing behind the desk clerk perks up when I say this. She leans over and takes the ticket from the clerk. "Ooh! I could use this, Marilyn, if you don't mind."

Marilyn shrugs.

"And—wait—you must be Emily!" the blond woman says.

"Uh, yes?" Do I know her? She does look a little familiar, although I'm not the best at remembering faces. She's wearing a name tag that says *Heidi Jo*. I'm sure I don't know anyone by that name.

"Oh, this is awesome. Have a good game!" She grins at me.

Puzzled, I thank her and head for the turnstiles.

Armed with a falafel and a beer, I make my way to row D. I'm so close to the ice that I can see every player's expression during warmups.

This is amazing. I can't believe Charles didn't want to come. I leave the aisle seat empty so that whoever arrives won't have to climb over me.

My seat is right above the Bruisers' bench, and I'm so close to the action that I'll be able to see the sweat on the players' faces.

Just before the game begins, the starters line up for the anthem. The rest of the team files into place on the bench, including staff.

James is the last man to step off the ice, in his purple Bruisers jacket, a toolbox in his hand, and several hockey sticks tucked under his arm. His eyes find me for the briefest of moments. I get a flicker of a smile before he files down the row, behind the bench, his back to me.

After the anthem, the game kicks off. I lean forward in my seat and forget about James. I forget about my fight with Charles. I forget everything except for the glory that is hockey.

The pricey seat next to mine sits empty for the first period, but at least I tried.

It's a good game, too. We're favored to win against Tampa, but the Florida team wants it badly. The speed of play is super-fast, and I can see *everything* from this vantage point.

Charles is crazy. Who wouldn't want more of this?

During the intermission, I realize that I've been too excited to eat. So I finish my falafel and my beer and hit the ladies' room.

I might be alone tonight, but I'm still having a great time. This is much more fun than kissing some stranger's ass in a SoHo art gallery.

After the second period starts, there is a brief flurry of activity beside me when someone arrives to sit in the empty seat.

It takes me a few minutes to even look at my new companion. Because hello, Brooklyn *scores*! I scream for Tankiewicz's goal, and Charles isn't here to silence me for it.

Eventually, though, I notice that people nearby are sneaking looks at the woman in the aisle seat. When I finally sneak my own glance at her, I find a dark-haired beauty beside me. She looks vaguely familiar.

Another woman, wearing an earpiece, arrives a moment later to hand her a bottle of beer, top still on, and a bottle opener.

"Thank you," the beauty says. She pops open the drink and hands back the opener and the bottle top.

Some people are eccentric. Whatever.

I turn my gaze back to the game, which is very exciting right now, as Tampa tries to answer our goal.

They almost get a goal of their own, too, but Silas Kelly deflects two in a row in a blur of speed.

"YES BABY!" yells the woman next to me. "CRUSH THAT REBOUND!"

He does. Then Trevi gets the puck back and breaks for our attack zone.

"That was close," the woman mutters. Someone brings her a box of popcorn. She seems to have a lot of helpers. It's weird.

And it gets even weirder when her bodyguard person brings her a strange collection of hockey programs, cards, and a hat. The woman pulls a Sharpie out of her bag and quickly signs all of them before handing them back and refocusing on the game.

I sneak another look at her, because I'm getting the feeling I should know who she is. But I don't. Unfortunately, she catches me staring.

"Um, are you someone important?" I stammer.

She laughs. "Everyone is someone important."

"Fair enough," I say, even though it doesn't always feel like the truth.

"And while we're on that topic, hold on." She digs into her bag again and comes out with a notebook. She opens the cover, then flips a couple of pages. "I have a few things to tell you about Jimbo."

Wait, what?

"Heidi Jo wanted me to emphasize that he has a heart of gold and a lot of friends, all of whom would lay down in the road for him," she says, consulting her notes. "Oh, and he's polite and generous. It also says here that he helps old ladies cross the street. But I can't be sure if that's literal or metaphorical." She raises her eyes to mine. "New goal in life—never become someone who needs help crossing streets."

"Right?" I laugh uncomfortably.

I'm about to ask several follow-up questions when I notice all the other fans leaning forward in their seats. Trevi has been fouled, giving Brooklyn a power play. Brooklyn is trying to capitalize.

And then—whoa! Bayer sneaks the puck past a Tampa sniper and onto Castro's stick.

Castro fires, and the lamp lights a split second later.

We're on our feet in Row D and screaming our lungs out. My new companion has really good lungs, actually. And when everything calms down, I sneak my phone out of my pocket and Google *Silas Kelly girlfriend*.

"Oh my god," I say when the results pop up. "You're Delilah Spark."

"All day long," she says, her eyes on the players.

"Did Jimbo ask you to talk to me?" I yelp.

"Well, no. Heidi Jo told Silas you were here, and Silas told me that Jimbo needed someone to put in a good word. But everyone else—Leo and Jason and Heidi—they all were on board. But not in a creepy way. Cross my heart."

I laugh nervously. "Okay, truth time. How well do you actually know Jimbo?"

She waves a hand. "We've met a few times."

"But you're willing to talk him up anyway?" Is it me, or is this whole encounter super weird?

"The team is like a big family," Delilah says. "Popcorn?" She offers the box to me.

"Uh, thanks." I take a few kernels just to be social.

"You know, if a guy has a lot of nice friends, he is probably a pretty good guy. It's a big fat clue. That's something I ignored for a long time, and I ended up regretting it. I didn't trust my gut enough." She turns to me. "I'm not the best person to give you advice, honestly. So you'll have to trust your gut, too."

Well, damn. Even as she says this, I realize my gut has been yelling a lot of things lately. And I haven't been listening to any of them.

But maybe I should start.

"Oh, and at the end of the game I'm supposed to give you this." She pulls a card out of her pocket. "But I'm afraid I'll forget. So here it is now."

The card is white plastic, with a magnetic stripe on it. *Emily* is written on it in marker. "What's this?"

"A backstage pass. In case you want to meet anyone downstairs in the locker corridor.

Gulp.

Brooklyn wins the game, 3-2, and I manage to catch James's eye one more time when he leaves the bench. He gives me a friendly wave and a wink.

"Aw, see?" Delilah says. "He's sweet on you. What a cutie."

I feel a little melty inside, because it's been such a long time since a boy tried to impress me. Flirting is completely foreign to me. No wonder I'm such a pushover.

Delilah gets up as her bodyguard beckons her to start moving toward the exit. "Coming downstairs?" she asks, pointing toward an elevator.

I shake my head. I can't go out for drinks with another man in the middle of a fight with Charles. That's just not right. So I thank her for her company tonight and take the subway home alone.

And, hey, when you're not experiencing anaphylactic shock, it's much easier to leave the stadium on your own power.

On my way, I picture Charles in Manhattan, trying to woo clients and secure his future. I doubt he was very interested in that art opening. He probably just wanted a friendly face there beside him.

He should have been more diplomatic about it, although I have some sympathy for his position. All his new responsibility at work? It's probably awkward as hell. And he never complains.

At home, I get ready for bed in the darkened apartment I share with my mom. After tucking myself in, I send him a text. *Look, I'm sorry I let you down tonight.*

It's a generous interpretation of our fight. But it leaves

room for him to be generous, too. And I need that right now. I need him to be sweet and remind me why we're a team.

His response only takes a minute to arrive.

Charles: *You should be sorry. You missed a great opportunity to enrich yourself with art.*

Okay.

Well.

That was not the sort of response I'd been looking for. I touch the icon to call him. And I can feel my temper rising.

"Hello," he says, and his voice is wary. Maybe he's already regretting that response. He ought to be.

"You know what?" I say without a greeting. "You always try to make me feel like I'm in training. As if I'm here looking for life tips on how to get ahead."

"Getting ahead is always my focus," he says.

"I *know* that," I snap. "God, I know. But what if I want more out of life than that?"

"But that *is* how you get more!"

"It's not," I insist. "Sometimes you can do things just for fun. Or just because *someone you love* thinks it's fun."

"I can't afford fun," he says. "Not yet. But there will be time for fun later. And I really need you to be onboard for the whole ride."

Tonight, I'm not onboard.

But saying so would bring me too close to a cliff that I'm afraid to jump off. So I mumble something conciliatory and tell him I need to go.

"Love you," he says as a sign-off.

I'm too grumpy to repeat it.

CHAPTER EIGHT

CORPORATE ZOMBIES OF DOOM

8

James

After the game, I wait, and I hope. But it doesn't look good.

"She's not out in the corridor with the families. I'm sorry," Heidi Jo tells me as I carry sticks to the van. Every time I duck outside to the loading dock, I look up and down the block, hoping to spot her.

But she never comes.

Instead, I get a very nice thank-you text the next day.

Emily: That was so much fun! Thank you for giving me a ticket.

James: You are welcome. No boyfriend at the game last night? Delilah said she was your date. She thanks you for turning in the extra ticket, BTW.

Emily: No boyfriend at the game. He was going to come, but then he bailed at the last minute.

I argue with myself for a good half hour before responding. Does she need my opinion? No. But, fuck it. I give it to her anyway.

James: Just saying—if you were my date, there's no way I'm bailing at the last minute. Unless the zombies got me. Did the zombies get your man?

Emily: You know what? His job in finance sometimes makes it feel that way. The corporate zombies of doom often have him tight in their clutches.

Now I feel like a dick. Her guy probably hadn't made it because he was called in to work. My own job has bonkers hours. There's a reason I'm still single.

James: I hope things get better for both of you.

Emily: That is really nice of you to say. And it bears repeating—I had a great time last night. Thank you! And now I'm off to study for finals.

James: Good luck with your exams! I'm available for pizza refueling should the need arise.

Emily: Thanks again!

That's it. That's all she writes.

I groan aloud.

"Got a problem, Jimbo?" O'Doul—the Bruisers' captain—walks into the sharpening room and squints at me.

"Not sure," I grumble, lifting his skate off the sharpener and checking the edge. "You're all set. Here." I pass both skates over to him.

"Is it woman trouble? I heard your girl came to the game alone."

Lord, the gossip in this place. "She was alone. But she's not my girl. There's still a boyfriend. I think? What do you suppose this means?" I hold up my phone for his inspection. "But don't you dare reply, or I'll order you the wrong stick for the game against Toronto."

"Easy, killer." He reads my texts with Emily. "She doesn't say why her boyfriend wasn't there."

"I noticed that."

"That means the puck is in play."

"Does it, though? She's dating some banker—the kind of guy who wears a nice suit and pays for expensive dinners."

"You can rock a suit as well as the next guy." He punches me in the shoulder. "Don't do that, Jimbo. Don't assume the other guy can outskate you. That just makes you a loser before you ever step out onto the ice."

"Stretchin' this hockey metaphor a little far, captain."

"Nah," he says. "No such thing as too much hockey. You gotta size up your opponent. Get low and hit him with your weight, yeah? Beat him at his own game. You think I got this far assuming the other guy could win the faceoff?"

"No sir," I admit.

"What does this girl want in a man?" He shrugs. "Just figure that out and be that guy. It will all work out for you."

At that, the man takes his skates and goes, leaving me plenty to think about.

———

After thinking it through, I realize O'Doul is right. I'm not done here. I've got more fight left in me. So I start making plans.

"Hey, Ari?" I stop O'Doul's fiancée in the hallway on the way to the massage-therapy treatment room. "You like to eat vegetarian, right?"

"Yeah, I try," she says. "Why?"

"What's a great Brooklyn restaurant for a meatless meal? Bonus points if it's near downtown, and if they deliver."

"Oh, step into my parlor," she says. "I'll make you a list of the best ones."

"You're a goddess, Ari."

"Just invite me to your wedding, kid."

That afternoon I walk into the weight room when it's crowded. "Hey guys, I'm here to shamelessly ask for favors."

"Sexual favors?" asks Drake from the weight bench. "Will you talk dirty to me in your New York accent?"

"Fugghedaboutit," I say, and the whole room laughs.

"What do you need, Jimbo?" Silas asks. "We kinda owe you after pranking your date the other night."

"Funny you should mention that. I am looking for extra comp tickets for home games. And I'd love for everyone to sign this." I hold up a copy of the season's program—the fancy one from the gift shop. "She's a fan."

"Give it here," Drake says. "I'll start."

I produce a handful of Sharpies and start my way around the room. Everyone signs on his own page.

Stay cool Emily! Drake writes. *Love, Neil Drake, friend of Jimbo's*.

"How rude am I allowed to be?" Castro asks when it's his turn.

"Not rude at all. Should I skip you?" I hold the program out of his reach.

"Nah, nah. I can be good. Give it here. I have a comp seat for next week, too." He signs the program.

"Thanks, man! I really appreciate it."

"Have faith, Jimbo. If this grumpy ass is capable of winning a woman's love, yours ought to be, too."

"I feel so inspired right now," I whisper.

"Oh, shut it." Castro signs with a flourish and grins at me. "Now go get your girl."

So, for the next few weeks I give it all I've got. I send her a ticket to every single home game.

Just one ticket, though. Her guy is on his own.

At first, she seemed a little unsure if she should accept them. *James—this is really generous. I don't want to put you out,* she'd written.

You're not, I'd assured her. *Players give me their extras. No money changed hands.*

That is a relief, she'd replied. *The face value of these tickets is very spendy.*

I don't do spendy, I'd admitted. *But you and I agreed that money isn't everything. I see every game from rink level, and I don't pay a thing. My dad is still unimpressed.*

Good point, she'd agreed. *Although at least your dad isn't hounding you for tickets.*

True! So will I see you for drinks after the game? That pass card doesn't expire. No pressure though.

I don't think I should, she'd immediately replied. *I just need a little time to get my head on straight. I've been making some changes. It hasn't been easy, but I'm getting to a better place.*

And now I've probably read that text a hundred times, trying to decide what it means. She said she's "making some changes." That could mean anything. It could mean she broke up with the boyfriend.

But it could also mean that she'd changed her socks.

Out of respect for the lady's wishes, I haven't pressed her on it. Even though I'm dying of curiosity.

Meanwhile, it's been fun to treat Emily to a good time. I get the feeling from our occasional communications that she's under a lot of stress, so it makes me happy to give her a free night out. Whenever she comes to a game, I try to let her know I'm paying attention. So far:

I've sent an intern to her seat with a program signed by the whole team.

I sent her a hot meal from one of those vegetarian restaurants that Ariana likes.

And last week I sent the team's mascot to her seat to take a photo with her. That picture of Emily hugging the Brooklyn Brown Bear is the lock screen on my phone now. She's laughing, her clear eyes full of joy.

James—that bear! she'd texted that night. *Hilarious. Thank you! I've had a really rough week, and I needed that laugh.*

And, yup, that's payback enough. I want Emily. But more than that, I want to make her happy. And yet here I stand in the dressing room before a game, wondering whether tonight could be the night she meets me for drinks.

It's January, and the season is going well. Last night's minor disaster against New Jersey was the only game we lost out of our last six.

Every man in this locker room wants a victory against Carolina, so there's a pleasant hum of energy as I check my toolkit. It's almost game time, and this is my last chance to add to my emergency stash of tape and sticks before heading out to the bench.

Emily is probably in her seat already.

Will tonight's post-game scenario play out any differently

for me? Probably not. Everyone in professional sports knows that you can't win 'em all.

"Let's go, men!" O'Doul calls. "Let's make Carolina cry."

There's a deafening shout in surround sound, and then the team files past me, heading for the chute.

"Good game, Jimbo," someone says as he passes by.

"Good game," I reply. I always get back-pats, butt-pats, and noogies at times like this. Like I'm some kind of mascot. It comes with the paycheck and the free drinks I'll get if we win.

Heidi Jo hurries up to me just as I'm ready to follow the last guy out. "The Eagle has landed!" she chirps. "I moved Emily's seat to Row D, and she arrived before warmups. So—it's go-time?"

"Yeah, buddy. Thanks for all you do." Heidi Jo is my self-appointed wingman.

"Don't mention it. Are we delivering anything to her seat tonight?"

Slowly, I shake my head. "I'm out of ideas."

"Aw, don't lose faith," she says. "You already made your point. She'll come around. I put her next to Delilah again tonight. Do you want me to text Delilah? Is there anything you want to say?"

I think about it for a second, and then shake my head again. "I've said all I can say. I told the girl how I feel. If she wants to stay with her banker, that's her choice."

"You're a great guy, Jimbo. She must be blind and crazy." She pats me on the head as I lean over to pick up my toolbox and then dashes off.

Emily is neither blind nor crazy, though. She's just not my girl.

I leave the dressing room behind, heading down the chute

and onto the ice. It's a good crowd tonight. The stands are already filling up at a fast pace.

Players whiz by me as I walk carefully across the slick surface. I glance up just before I reach the door to the bench and train my eyes on Row D.

And there she is. My heart gives an embarrassing little lurch as I find Emily's pretty face in the crowd. She smiles at me. And—wait—she's holding up a small, hand-lettered sign.

BEHIND EVERY GREAT PLAYER THERE'S A GREAT BUTT PAD*

I snort before I even notice the footnote.

*AND A GREAT EQUIPMENT MANAGER

"Aw, look who's got his own fans!" Henry, the trainer, chirps. "Isn't that special?" He stands up on the bench and snaps a photo of Emily's sign.

Naturally, that prompts a few players to turn and look.

"Omigod, Jimbo!" Drake hoots. "You're so gettin' in there later."

"*Shush*," I grunt. "Or I'll replace your red glucose juice with the purple flavor again." One of my many jobs is to keep our resident Type 1 diabetic supplied with sugar boosts on the bench.

"Harsh," he complains.

"Then shut it." But the truth is that I'm secretly charmed by Emily's sign. It's totally worth catching a little hell.

It's got to mean something, right? Maybe tonight is the night she'll agree to date me. "Guys, please win this thing. I need to impress a girl."

O'Doul steps off the ice with a snort. "Hear that, boys? I don't care what motivates you tonight. Maybe it's Jimbo's dry spell. Maybe it's my grumpy face. But I want two goals in the first period. Let's shake 'em up out there."

Unfortunately, though, we do *not* get two goals in the first period. Carolina gets them, instead.

Coach Worthington looks apoplectic during the intermission. "Come on, guys. We can't have these missed opportunities! They're making you look bad in front of a hometown crowd. There's no reason for this."

As I rush around, replacing skate laces and handing out tape, I see a lot of determined faces. We've come back from worse. And every man in this room knows it.

"Um, Jimbo?" Heidi says, as I stash more tape in my tool kit. "I have some news." She holds up her phone and smiles.

"News?"

"Just got a text from Delilah. Emily told her that she broke up with the banker boyfriend."

"WHOA!" Drake says, clapping slowly. "Jimbo! Shit just got real."

Suddenly, all the players are hooting and hollering at me.

My face is red, and I'm not really sure why. And what does it all mean? "Come on," I growl. "Don't you guys have a game to win?"

"Let's do this, men!" Trevi calls, pointing toward the chute. "We can still do this. Let's end Jimbo's dry spell, guys. Win it for Jimbo!"

"Oh, please," I snort. "I'm more worried about the mood at your place tonight if we can't answer those lost goals. You think Georgia will be happy throwing another sad press conference after the game?"

Leo opens his mouth and then closes it again. There's a smattering of laughter.

"Let's impress some women," I grumble. "Or men. Whatever. Let's win this thing. Just do it before Coach bursts a vessel."

"You heard the kid," Coach barks. "Win it, already."

"Win it!" someone else yells. And they all go charging toward the ice.

I follow them a couple of minutes later, taking my place behind the bench without a glance at Row D. I can't think about Emily or Heidi Jo's little announcement. Emily will either tell me her news, or she won't. Nothing has changed for me.

And yet something has changed out on the ice. Three minutes into the period, Drake gets the first goal of the night, with an assist from O'Doul. After that, my guys start putting more pressure on our opponents.

We're down by one after the second period, but faces aren't so long anymore. This thing is winnable. And Carolina looks sluggish at the start of the third period. O'Doul and Bayer play an elaborate game of keep-away against our opponent's forwards, wearing them down.

Then Trevi decides to make something happen. He fires a saucer at the goal, but the keeper manages to bat it away.

"C'mon!" I shout as the puck flies off at a crazy angle.

"Rebound, baby," Wilson says in front of me. "Yeah!"

Castro flies toward the puck, slipping it onto his stick. He dumps it to O'Doul and then sets up again, looking for a better angle.

Then everything goes sideways as an opposing D-man tries a clumsy check on Castro. It's only half successful. Castro avoids getting flung into the boards, but his stick gets tangled between his opponent's legs and snaps.

The next ten seconds happen at warp speed. But I'm still going to remember it for the rest of my life.

My hand grabs for a replacement stick even as I climb up

onto the bench, my feet on either side of Wilson's generously sized ass.

"What the hell, Jimbo?" Wilson says as my knees hug his back.

But I'm not paying him any attention at all. Castro is flying toward me as I lean over Wilson like a circus performer on top of a pyramid, dangling the stick over the ice.

Castro's gloved hand wraps around the shaft just as the puck comes flying in his direction. The whole stadium holds its breath as Castro lowers his new stick to the ice to receive it. One-handed.

I lift my head at the same split second that Castro lifts his. We both see the net—and the clean, clear opening between Castro and a goal. It's like a goddamn tunnel of light. Couldn't be more obvious unless there was an angel hovering above it, beckoning to us.

Castro doesn't even hesitate. He fires a shot so fast I barely see his arm move. A millisecond later, the lamp lights.

"Yes!" screams the entire stadium.

The whole bench jumps to their feet, including Wilson, and I almost fall ingloriously to the floor from the sudden disruption. But I shoot a hand out and catch the plexi behind me, instead.

"JIMBO!" O'Doul hollers, skating past us. "You saved the game, man!"

Stunned, I hop down from the bench, and the whole team converges on my body. Wilson wraps his arms around my waist and hoists me into the air, while the rest of them surge into a very tight, very sweaty group hug.

"Uh, guys," I gasp. "No padding, here."

Laughing, Wilson sets me down. "Christ, I can't wait to see

the video. Musta been less than one second between you handin' off that stick and the goal."

"We'll clock it," someone says. "There's an app on my phone for that."

I just laugh. It's only dawning on me that the video will, indeed, be awesome. I get about thirty fist bumps in thirty seconds, which is a lot, seeing as there's only twenty guys dressed for the game. And the DJ is blasting Satriani's "Crowd Chant" to rile up the fans.

Then the announcer calls the play. "Goal by Jason Castro. Assist goes to James Carozza."

Wait. Maybe I need my ears cleaned out, because it sounded like he said my name.

The bench erupts into cheers again.

I can't believe that just happened.

Did that really just happen?

Either way, I'm wearing a smile so big you could keep a hockey bag in there. And it occurs to me that Emily might be watching. Slowly, I turn around.

She's on her feet, staring right at me, one hand pressed to her mouth, the other gripping Delilah's arm. They're both jumping up and down like two little girls at a birthday party.

Emily stops jumping when she sees me watching. She drops her hand and gives me a shy smile.

This is my big chance. A man can sense these things. So I lift my hand, and I blow her a kiss.

Then I say a silent prayer as I turn around again. *Send me a sign, girl.* Love me or leave me.

And please let it be that first thing.

CHAPTER NINE

CAN'T BELIEVE THAT JUST HAPPENED

9

Emily

I can't believe that just happened. James made that goal possible. They even said so over the stadium airwaves.

It's a hockey miracle, and I witnessed it. I'm so happy for him I could spit.

Okay, forget spitting. I pull my wallet out of my pocket and open it up. The backstage pass is still there, between my metro card and my student ID. I've kept it there since the day Delilah handed it to me.

"They don't expire," James had said. But that's only partly true. Opportunities don't last. People move on.

James just had a big night—a career-making night. If I don't see him face to face—and thank him for letting me be a part of that—then I can't really accept any more tickets from him. It just wouldn't be fair of me. I won't want to string along a great guy just because I'm kind of a mess.

Breaking up with Charles last weekend was a really difficult thing to do. It was a long time coming. But I am not in love with him anymore. We want different things.

That doesn't mean I'm ready to date another guy, though.

On the other hand, I *have* to celebrate with James, right? It's his big night. It's now or never.

That's what I'm going to tell myself, anyway.

Though, I already know what will happen if I do. That boy will kiss me. And I'll let him. He'll ask me out on another date, and I'll probably say yes.

I've been single for five whole days. Before that, I hadn't been single since middle school. But I've promised myself I won't be anyone else's doormat again or arrange my life around a man's.

These deep thoughts are interrupted by another goal against Carolina. Delilah shoots out of her seat, and I'm right there with her. We scream for Leo Trevi, who just brought us into the lead.

"This is *such* a great game," Delilah gushes.

"Yes!" I agree as we sit back down. "The best game." Just hanging out with a rock star here in row D. No big deal, right?

"Your guy must be walking on air," she says.

"He's not really my guy," I admit.

"Just keep telling yourself that," she says. "The women will swarm him tonight. After that play? Just saying."

Something goes wrong in my stomach.

Delilah chuckles. "You should see your face right now, girly. Better get in there before someone else does."

She makes a few good points.

It's only a drink, I tell myself as I pull out the phone. *It doesn't have to be a big deal.*

Tell that to my shaking hands as I send him a text.

YOU GOT AN ASSIST! OMG. You should have heard me and Delilah screaming. I was like I KNOW THAT GUY.

I add a smiley face and then I plunge ahead. *Can I buy you a drink to celebrate? I'm going to use the white card to try to find you. If that doesn't work, I'll look for the van out back. Unless you're busy. Let me know!*

Well, I was trying for breezy. The result was about as smooth as an eighth-grader asking a boy if he's going to the middle-school dance. But in my defense, I was in the eighth grade the last time I was single.

This is hard. No wonder I spent so many years with Charles. It's easier to accept the status quo than to get out there and get my flirt on.

I shove my phone back into my pocket and watch the rest of the game. Carolina already looks beaten, even with a few minutes left on the clock. They don't manage to answer Trevi's goal, either.

When the final buzzer sounds, we are victorious once again. Delilah's handlers scurry down to get her, as usual.

"Before you go," I say quickly. "Where do I go to find James with this?" I hold up the card.

She beams. "Follow us, toots. I'll show you."

I haven't seen James up close for over a month. So when he comes out into the crowded hallway to fetch me, I'm a little overwhelmed at the sight of him. Was he always this tall and strapping? Were his eyes always that deep shade of brown, his lashes so long and devastating?

"Emily," he says in a low voice. "Hey. Did you enjoy the game?"

"Are you *kidding* me right now? It was the most exciting thing ever. I texted you after your assist. I'm hoarse from screaming."

He flashes me a hot smile. "Come to the Tavern with us tonight? If you aren't there to save me, these guys are going to get me *very* drunk. It will be, uh, another half hour until I can leave, though."

"That's okay," I say quickly. "Where should I wait?"

"Come with me," he says, hooking his arm in mine.

I'm probably beaming as he leads me quickly through a door marked DRESSING ROOM.

And—holy crap—the label is not wrong. I try not to stare as we cross the room amid half-naked players and a whole lot of sports reporters. And oh my God, there's Anton Bayer's bare bottom! There's a tattoo of the Brooklyn Bridge on it!

I force my eyes to look away as we cross through to the outer chamber where the coat lockers are. I was here the night of my allergic reaction. James shows me to a wooden bench. "Hang here for a few? I have to carry a few things to the van."

"Can I be of any help?" I ask.

His smile is amused. "No, sweetheart. But thanks for asking." Then? He leans right down and kisses my cheek, before walking quickly out of the room.

I just stare after him, his muscular ass a sight in faded jeans. And I think I might be drooling a little.

Keep it together, Chen, I coach myself. *He's just a guy.*

But what a guy. Big and strong. Polite. And so handsome that I get a little stupid when we're in the same room together. If he actually kisses me tonight, I might stroke out.

Sitting here and waiting for him is less boring than you'd think. The people-watching is spectacular. Players filter through in ones and twos, opening their lockers to retrieve their suit jackets and coats. "Coming to the Tavern?" Castro asks Drake.

"Sure, man. Uber or walk?"

"Uber."

I wonder if Uber drivers get starstruck when they pick up hockey players outside the stadium. I'm willing to bet they do.

Wilson comes out and dons his coat. It probably takes a whole herd of sheep to make a topcoat that wide. Then he notices me sitting here. "Hey, it's Emily!"

My face heats. Wilson remembers my *name*? "Hi. Thanks again for your help that night last fall."

"No problem." I expect him to walk right by me, but he sits down on the bench. "You doing okay? Any more reactions?"

"I've been fine," I tell him. "No more reactions. But changing my diet was a big adjustment."

"Meat, huh?" he asks with a shake of his head. "I can't imagine. There's only so much chicken and fish a guy can eat."

"It's okay," I insist. "I never ate that much meat anyway. But it…" I wonder if he really wants to hear this, or if he's just being polite. "I'm constantly nervous about triggering it again. It's made eating into a scary adventure that I never wanted to have." I laugh, like this is funny. But it comes out sounding a little hysterical.

"Hey." He puts a hand on my arm. "I'm sorry to hear that. Some people get real bad PTSD about this."

"It's not *that* bad," I say quickly.

He lifts his giant eyebrows. "Does it interfere with you eating? Have you lost weight?"

I shake my head slowly. "I'm eating. I just don't, uh, enjoy it much anymore."

"That's a shame, girl. You have your own epi now?"

"Oh, of course," I concede. "I take it everywhere I go."

"Good," he says. "The thing is? That stuff *works*. I know you're spooked. I know you don't want to feel those symptoms again. But you're going to be all right. Really. Live large and carry epi, okay?"

"Okay," I say as his eyes crinkle with a smile.

He stands up. "Coming to the Tavern with us?"

"Think so."

He lifts his big paw, and it takes me a second to figure out that I'm supposed to high five him. And I do.

"See ya there, Emily. Jimbo will be psyched, you know. He's been workin' it pretty hard, yeah?"

"Um…" It's hard to know what to say to that.

"If you're into him, put that boy out of his misery." He gives me another grin and lopes toward the door.

———

Before tonight, I'd never been to the Tavern on Hicks. The bar is not fancy, or particularly interesting, except for the fact that more than half of Brooklyn's winningest team is drinking here.

What's more, James's big moment is playing on repeat on the big screen over the bar. We haven't paid for a drink all night. The players keep refilling our beer glasses, and I've seen James do two or three shots.

And yet he's still rock solid. His palm is a steady presence on my lower back—warm, but not handsy. His eyes are still bright and easy, as every member of the team—and a dozen strangers—offer congratulations one by one.

"What a night you're having." I set down my beer glass because I don't want anyone to refill it again. "How does it feel to be suddenly famous?"

"It feels *late*," he says, checking the time. "Do you have school tomorrow? I should get you home."

"It's Saturday?"

"Sorry." He laughs. "This job will make you forget what day of the week it is. Hockey is 24/7."

"I've had enough to drink, though. I should probably get home. But you don't have to go if you're having fun."

"No, I'm good." He puts his glass on the bar next to mine, and my stomach flutters. "Let's ride."

He says good night to a few guys, and then I follow him outside, my heart thumping. He strolls up to the curb, puts two fingers into his mouth and whistles. Two seconds later, a taxi slides up to the curb in front of him. He opens the rear door, then turns around, waiting for me.

I slide into the backseat, as if it's preordained that we should share a cab.

He gets in and then speaks to the driver. "We're heading to Bensonhurst. Thanks, man."

"You don't have to go all the way out there," I say in an unsteady voice. "If it's out of the way for you."

"There's something you don't know about me," he says, relaxing against the headrest. "I live on East Nineteenth in Midwood."

"Oh." I laugh. "Really?" That's so close to me.

"Hand to God," he says, holding up a palm. "So it's not out of the way."

The cab slides away from the curb, and then it's just James and me together in the backseat, alone with my thumping heart.

"Thank you for coming out with me tonight," he says quietly.

"Well, I've always wanted to," I admit. "But I feel like I met you at exactly the wrong time."

"That's funny," he says. "Because I feel like I met you at exactly the right time."

"Why is that?"

He shrugs. "Because any time with you is the right time."

Those smooth words make me take a slow blink. I'm not used to hearing romantic notions like that. And I'm *definitely* not used to the way this man reaches across, takes my hand in his, and kisses my knuckles.

"James?" I squeak.

"Yeah, sweetheart?"

"I broke up with the banker. I've been meaning to for a while, now. But it took me a long time to get the courage to actually do it."

He turns his body so he can look me in the eye. "I was wondering if you were going to bring that up."

And now my cheeks are on fire. "You heard? *Already?* Just because I mentioned it to Delilah?"

"My friends live for gossip," he says with a smile, his dark eyes twinkling. "Probably only took five minutes to get to Heidi Jo and then to me."

"Wow," I whisper. And still, I don't even know why I told him, or exactly what I want him to do about it.

"If you didn't bring it up, I wasn't going to say anything," he says in a low voice. "But since you did bring it up…"

I wait for him to finish the sentence. He does, but not in words. He clasps my hand and gives me a gentle tug in his direction. I go easily. Willingly. His first kiss is soft and slow. A graceful snick of his lips, with a thumb swept across my wrist with aching sweetness.

And I am already won over to the James Carozza experience as he tilts his head to kiss me again. I lean in, wanting more, and he makes a soft sound of approval as his mouth teases mine a second time, and then a third.

He's the second man I've *ever* kissed. I'm a little shocked at how different it feels. The scruff on his face is new, as is the broadness of his body as he eases me against his big chest.

Honestly, it's his hunger that I find the most shocking. I hadn't realized that hands could be gentle but still needy. His fingertips skate up the back of my jacket with energy and wonder. The tilt of his head is tender but so damn focused. And when he tastes the seam of my mouth with his tongue, I find myself softening immediately for him. I want to taste that hunger on my tongue.

He doesn't make me wait. He plunders my mouth, and then he lets out a groan that somehow manages to be constrained and urgent at the same time.

The car takes a corner, and the momentum tries to lurch my body away from James. He steadies me instantly. Still, I reach up to hold onto more of him. The solid bulk of his shoulders is another shock. I'm kissing a heated giant of a man in the back of a taxi.

I like it. A lot.

But then he breaks our kiss. "Come home with me," he whispers.

CHAPTER TEN

MY OVERHEATED
LITTLE BRAIN

10

Emily

Come home with me.

His words hang between us, and for a moment I just stare at him, stunned at the forwardness of this request.

It's not that I think there's anything wrong with two adults running off together to tear off each other's clothes if they feel like it. But I'm not used to being that woman. I haven't shown my naked body to anyone new in... ever. There was only Charles. And we'd known each other for so long by the time we finally had sex that the event itself was anticlimactic.

Literally.

Seconds tick by while my overheated little brain tries to process this idea. James is waiting for my answer, his brown eyes boring into mine.

"Well..." I say, truly conflicted and more than a little intimidated.

James dips his handsome chin and kisses my neck. Goosebumps immediately break out all over my body. Oh boy. It's really hard to think when he does that. I grip his shoulders and let out a shivery breath.

He chuckles. "It's okay, Emily. I'll take you home."

"But—" I argue, even though I feel relieved to hear him say that so easily. "If I say no, does that mean you won't ever ask again?" Because that would be a tragedy.

"No way." He lifts his head to study me solemnly. "I'll ask again," he whispers. "You can bet on it."

"Oh," I say stupidly, as James's arms scoop me off the seat and deposit me on his lap. Now we're nose to nose. His arms encircle me, and he gives me a kiss on the forehead.

He studies me some more, his gaze like a caress. I can actually feel the heat of it on my skin. I take his face in both of my hands, and his scruff tickles my palms. "You are ridiculously attractive. It's really not fair."

He grins, changing the shape of his face in my hands. "Back atcha, sweetheart."

A glance out the window shows me Sixtieth Street, and I realize that my time with him is almost finished.

And, wow, that is just unacceptable. Suddenly I don't want to go home. I don't want to pierce the perfect bubble, where there's only James and me. And, well, a taxi driver.

"Excuse me, sir?" I hear myself say through the gap in the partition. "Can you take us to East Nineteenth Street instead?"

"East Nineteenth and...?"

"Foster," James says immediately. It comes out a little like "Fostah," the edges of his Brooklyn accent breaking through.

"You got it."

James smooths my hair away from my face. "You sure?" he whispers.

"Yes," I insist. "I'm just, um, not good at this."

The grin he gives me is so very James—wicked and sweet at the same time. "At what, exactly?"

"Um… Dating." *And seduction. Flirting. Everything.*

"You're doing just fine," he whispers. Those brown eyes flash, and then somehow we're kissing again.

Only now that I'm seated in his lap, it's more of a full-body experience. Like a very exciting amusement park ride, where anything might happen—such as his tongue in my mouth and his hand squeezing my bottom. His thumb brushing over my nipple, sensitive despite several layers of fabric in the way.

My arousal is swift and all-consuming, in a way I haven't felt in a long time. I'm basically one lit match shy of an open flame by the time the cab comes to a halt. I find myself placed gently onto the seat, while James pays the cabbie.

Cool air hits my heated face as I exit the taxi on wobbly knees. James follows me, telling the cabbie to keep the change.

"Thanks, man. You have fun tonight." The driver's voice is amused, and I feel a wave of embarrassment at having gotten carried away in the back of a taxi at two in the morning.

Who even am I right now?

James shuts the door without comment, parks a hand at the small of my back, and leads me around the corner, onto Nineteenth Street. I've seen these streets before, since we're only about ten blocks from my own apartment building.

Midwood is just on the other side of Mapleton from Bensonhurst, where I live, but this block looks completely different from my own. Instead of apartment buildings, there are stately, old, three-story Victorian-era homes, with driveways between them and lawns in front and back. I always marveled at these houses as a little girl. They looked like the homes I saw on television.

"Nice neighborhood," I say as we walk past a couple houses on the silent street.

"I rent from my aunt," he explains. "The cost is super low, and I'm invited for dinner every Sunday that I'm in town. Although I do mow the lawn."

"Seems like a great deal. Is your aunt a good cook?"

"The best. Sunday dinner is a big feast. I'm sad to miss it when we're traveling." He wraps an arm around my shoulders. "We're just over here."

The driveway where we turn leads to the rear of a wide house painted a dark color. Blue, I think. There's a bay window in front and porches that stretch the width of both the first and second floors.

As we head toward the garage, an exterior set of stairs comes into view. "It's a bit of a climb," he says, stepping aside to let me go first.

Gripping the wooden railing, I climb the first few stairs. James follows, his heavier tread making the wood creak.

It's the middle of the night, and I'm climbing a secluded staircase to a man's room. Nobody knows where I am. At all. There are probably scary movies that begin like this.

And yet the thumping of my heart is one hundred percent nervous anticipation, not true fear. I feel safe with this man, if a little overwhelmed by him.

On the landing, he pulls a heavy set of keys from his pocket and uses one to open the door. "It's not much, but it's home."

We enter the apartment, and he quickly walks to the corner of the room to turn on a lamp. I see a large space with slanting ceilings and cute dormer windows. One half is taken up by the spacious attic bedroom of my girlhood dreams, although it's finished with a manly grey flannel comforter on the big four-poster bed. The other half is a small living area with a sofa, a coffee table, and the kind of tiny, barely functional kitchen that you can only find in the five boroughs of New York City.

"I kind of love it," I say stupidly. "And you're a very tidy man, James."

He chuckles. "This is what it looks like when you're almost never home." He removes my coat as smoothly as a Bridgerton valet and hangs it on a coat rack beside the door.

The man is seriously tidy, even if he can't take a compliment. I watch him hang up his own coat and set his shoes on a rack against the wall.

I'm sort of frozen near the door, unsure what to do. Now that the kissing has stopped, I don't know my role here.

James comes closer. He puts his hands on my upper arms and gives a gentle squeeze. "Can I get you a drink?"

It's tempting to say yes, but a drink would only prolong my nervous anxiety. We both know why I'm here. It would be silly to pretend otherwise.

Slowly, I shake my head.

"Well, all right, then." He bends his knees and scoops an arm under my knees, picking me up off the floor.

I let out a squeak of surprise as he holds me against his body and stalks toward the bedroom. Then I go absolutely quiet as his smile begins to drop generous kisses on my neck. It seems that all I've got left to say is a full-body shiver.

A moment later, my back hits the mattress. James spreads his big body out over mine, and we're at it again, with deep, dark kisses. The taste of him is already my new favorite drug.

I guess we'll be skipping the awkward chit-chat, and I'm fine with that. I melt back against his bed and enjoy every kiss, every deep delve of his tongue into my mouth.

And *good grief*, he's good at this. I never knew it was possible to be polite and bossy at the same time, but James is a study in contrasts. His touch is firm, yet gentle, as he unbuttons my blouse with confident fingers. Then he reaches behind my back and unhooks my bra more smoothly than I could do it myself.

He is, after all, an equipment manager. This is basically his specialty.

Lucky for me, each newly revealed patch of skin receives kisses and caresses. His mouth takes a slow, decadent tour of my breasts, while I arch and pant and generally make a fool of myself. I weave my fingers into his thick hair and marvel at the way he makes every experience brand new again.

I mean—I've been touched before. But I've never been *worshiped* quite like this. His lips are taking a victory tour of my upper body, and the soft sounds of appreciation he's making are more than I deserve.

Eventually, James pulls back. I'm disappointed until he calmly dispenses with my jeans and shoes.

Just wow.

My mind is staticky fuzz, although I'm aware that I should probably be participating more avidly. I gather the fabric of his shirt in my fingers and give a tug.

But no. James takes my hands and moves them back to the comforter, one at a time, as if to say *wait here, please and thank you.*

I grip the fabric, my hips twisting eagerly as the soft flannel finds more and more of my skin. James works the last of my clothing off, and then I'm completely bared to him on the bed.

My heart crashes against my ribs as he makes a low noise of appreciation. He's staring down at my naked body, and I'd be feeling self-conscious if the heat in his gaze wasn't burning away all my fear.

Filled with unfamiliar excitement, I lift a hand and beckon to him.

He grins, and at first, I'm not sure he'll obey my summons. But then his thick fingers move to the buttons of his shirt, and a moment later I get my first look at his muscular chest.

Lord, he's like a superhero, with a sixpack and a line of trimmed black hair that descends from his abdomen into his pants.

My mouth actually waters. "Let me," I say, and it comes out breathy as I sit up. "Please?"

I reach for his fly.

CHAPTER ELEVEN

GOD IS A BRUISERS FAN

11

James

I don't know what I did right in life that made this perfect moment possible. Somehow I must have pleased a higher power. That's the only explanation for why Emily is unbuttoning my fly and unzipping me.

Maybe God is a Bruisers fan. That must be it.

I hold perfectly still, breathing through my arousal. It's been a long time since I've been this turned on.

Emily seemed a little skittish on our way over here, and I'd never want to rush her. The truth is that I'd wait any length of time for this. For her.

She's not making me wait right now, though. She reaches into my boxer briefs and wraps her hand around my cock.

My breath stutters, and at the sound of my struggle, her dark eyes dart up to mine. They're wondering what I'm going to do next.

Slowly, I let out my breath, and I clench my hands into fists. "You're killing me. You know that?"

Then she smiles, and I can see her relax. Shoulders easing, she strokes her thumb across my cockhead, which almost kills me. Meanwhile, that smile plays on her gorgeous mouth.

My body is wired with tension and sweet anticipation. *Lord, give me patience.* I unclench one of my fists and reach down to smooth Emily's silken hair with my palm. I force my muscles to relax. It isn't just for her sake. I don't want to rush through any of this experience.

She leans in and kisses my stomach, and I cradle her smooth face against my body, stroking the nape of her neck. She hums softly against my skin, kissing her way toward my happy trail and then rubbing her soft cheek against my belly, like a friendly cat.

"Mmm," I hear myself say as I get a lock on my self-control again.

She tugs down the elastic of my briefs and frees my cock completely. "Oh geez," she whispers, and my stomach pulses with a chuckle.

I'm just taking another deep breath when she slips her lips over my tip and takes me against her tongue. *Aw, hell.* That's good. No—that's *magic.* My abs clench as she uses her palm to slowly pump my shaft, while she sucks on my cockhead.

A hot gasp escapes my chest, and my fingers tighten in her hair.

She glances up at me again, and the sight of her taking my cock with lips stretched wide does nothing for my self-control. Her naked body undulates beneath me, and the view is almost too much.

But I'm a glutton for this kind of torture. So I widen my stance, shove down my trousers and briefs, and guide her hand to my balls, which are tight with arousal.

Her mouth is eager, and I throw back my head and close

my eyes. She works me over, slowly inching me toward the edge of my climax.

She moans, and the sound threatens to wreck me. "Enough, sweetheart," I bite out. As I withdraw, the loss of sensation makes me groan.

Emily sits back on her heels, pupils blown, lips wet and swollen. She looks a little shellshocked. In a good way.

I kick off the remainder of my clothing and then lie down on my back. "Come here." I crook my finger as she turns around to face me.

I reach for the bedside table and remove a condom from the drawer and hand it to her, just to make sure she's onboard.

She opens the pouch and takes out the condom. She offers it to me. "You'd better, um, do the honors."

So I do, while she watches me with reverent eyes.

"Come closer, sweetheart," I rasp. I grasp her hips and lift her until she's straddling me.

For the first time since we walked in the door, she looks hesitant. That won't do at all.

"Up here," I whisper, beckoning again.

She leans down to kiss me, and I draw her in, wrapping my arms around her warmth and kissing her with all I've got.

That does the trick. Emily relaxes against my chest. After I give her a thorough reminder of how much we need each other, she's practically purring in my arms. I tug her hips up my chest. At first, she doesn't take the hint. She's too busy kissing me.

One more tug breaks our kiss. I slide her body up my torso, forcing her to grab the headboard as I pull my prize towards my mouth.

"Oh," she gasps, finally taking my meaning. "Oh, I couldn't possibly—"

However that sentence was supposed to end, I don't hear it.

I hear a long, helpless moan, instead.

Emily

Oh.

Oh boy.

Oh, sweet heaven.

All I can do is lean over the headboard and let out another moan. James holds me by the hips, suspended over his mouth. His wicked, beautiful mouth. The same tongue that always speaks so politely is rapidly driving me into a frenzy.

This is neither sweet nor polite, and I love every second of it. My climax—usually so elusive—is rushing toward me. I can tell. But a moment before it hits, James lifts my hips and backs off.

I look down at him, stunned and practically dizzy with need. He looks right back up at me and *smiles*.

Honestly, sexual disappointment is pretty familiar to me. So it takes my poor little brain a second to realize that this is all intentional. James is playing my body like a fiddle.

I let out a frustrated groan, and he makes a noise of deep satisfaction. Then he lowers me to his mouth and sucks gently. The sound of it is just about the most wonderfully dirty thing I've ever heard. I drop my head and float on the pleasure of it all.

Later, I'll probably blush just remembering this, but I can't resist moving against his mouth. My climax is so nearby. It's right there. It's...

He lifts me off his body again, and I let out an anguished gasp. How *dare* he? I'm opening my mouth to protest, when he lifts his hips a good two feet off the bed and fills me in one smooth, overwhelming motion.

My body spasms around his girth, and my shout of protest turns into a moan so loud that it echoes off the slanted ceiling.

Destabilized by surprise, I start to fall onto his body. My hands land heavily on his muscular shoulders, while I try to get my bearings.

He doesn't wait. James's face is a sexy grimace as he bites his lip and pumps his hips in an ancient rhythm.

Looking down, I see the hottest view I've *ever* had, as his abs flex and bunch. So hot that it pushes me over the edge. A wave of bliss rolls up from my toes, flowing through me as I shudder and moan.

He pulls me down onto his chest and kisses me through it as I shamelessly flex my hips, wringing every last drop of pleasure from my body.

I flop down on his chest, spent.

"Christ almighty," he whispers. "You're spectacular." He rolls us both over and kisses me again, his hard body straining against mine. I lift my tired legs and hug his hips with my knees.

He drops one more blistering kiss on my lips and lets out a half grunt, half moan, before shuddering his release. Then he collapses onto my body with a laugh.

I run my fingers through his hair and try not to pant too loudly. When even that seems like too much work, I drop my jellyfish arms to the bed and exhale.

"Well," he says eventually. "Swear to God I meant to kiss you goodnight and ask you out on a real date. Didn't mean to drag you back to my lair and have my filthy way with you. Not tonight, anyway. I was gonna save that for later."

I find my voice. "Glad you didn't. Tonight was amazing." It's a revelation, if I'm honest. I thought I wasn't the kind of girl who could decide to just go home with a guy for sex.

The truth is more complicated, I guess. Who knows what kind of girl I might be? And how do you *ever* figure that out if you date the same boy since middle school?

"You okay?" James asks, running a hand up my thigh.

"I'm great," I assure him. "Never better."

Several hours later, I wake up to the sound of pounding on a door. Not *my* door. As my eyes fly open, I'm startled to find myself naked in bed.

James's bed.

The night's wild events come rushing back to me—like James's big moment at the game. Then drinking beer with the greatest hockey team of all time, James's hand at the small of my back. And making out in the taxi.

And earth-shattering sex.

After that came even more sex in James's shower, leading me to wonder whose exciting life I'd stumbled into by accident.

We'd finally fallen into bed around four a.m. But now his apartment is flooded in sunlight, and someone is pounding on the door.

"Jimmy! Can you open this jar of pickles?"

He groans. "Just a second Aunt Luna."

"Can I come in?"

I yank the sheet up over my naked body in panic.

"Not on your life," he says, sitting up.

Aunt Luna lets out a comical laugh.

"My ears," James complains. He grabs sweatpants and a T-shirt from a dresser and pulls them on.

"Should I come back later?" She cackles through the door. "Was hoping to put a pickle in your uncle's lunch."

"Gimme a sec. I'll come down to the kitchen."

"Thank you."

James comes back and sits on the edge of the bed. He puts a broad hand on my tummy. "Sorry about that."

"What time is it?" I ask, half afraid of the answer.

"Almost ten?" He chuckles. "Don't go anywhere, okay? I'll be right back. You drink coffee?"

"I *live* for coffee."

"Then don't move." He leans over and kisses my forehead. "I gotta open some pickles, take my teasing, but then I'll come right back."

He lets himself out and disappears, and then I sit up and take stock.

James's snug apartment is even more appealing in the daylight. His bedroom area is set apart by a set of pocket doors that I hadn't noticed last night, because they're wide open. There are white curtains at the windows, and a set of framed family photos arranged on one wall.

It's homey and more charming than I'd expect from a single man in his twenties.

I, however, look less charming in the harsh light of day. My clothes are scattered all around the bedroom, and I do a strange little dance of shame trying to quickly pluck my underwear off the wood floor and pull them on before he can return to witness it.

That accomplished, my next priority is the crazy sex hair I

see in the bathroom mirror. I quickly rake it into a bun and secure it with a clip from my bag. I also have a toothbrush in there, from nights spent at Charles's place.

I feel a stab of guilt just thinking of Charles. I push the thought away and grab the tube of Crest off the vanity.

I hear the apartment door open as I'm brushing my teeth. "Emily?"

"In here!" I say, turning on the water to spit.

I'm leaning over the sink when a warm hand lands on my bare back. "For a second there I thought you'd hightailed it." He runs a finger up my spine as I turn off the faucet.

"I was just trying to make myself more presentable." I turn around and drop my toothbrush back into its tube.

His eyes take in my travel toothbrush, but he doesn't say anything.

"I always carry this," I insist.

He grins. "Ah, well. You're hard on my ego, Emily."

"There's no way that's true," I say.

"If you say so." His shrug suggests that I'm wrong, but he doesn't want to argue.

And that's a revelation, too. "Honestly? I'd just assumed you could have anyone you wanted. With your sexy job, and your...well..." I make a vague gesture at his body. His incredible, sculpted body with that gorgeous face on top of it.

Again, he grins. "Come and have coffee with me, okay? The only girl I want is the one wearing her undies in my bathroom."

When I emerge, there's a two-handled tray on the tousled bed. On the tray are two steaming cups of coffee, a creamer, a sugar bowl, and two homemade-looking muffins.

Someone pinch me. James can't even be real.

After coffee and a fantastic homemade muffin, I know it's time to go. "Let me get out of your hair," I tell James. "Where are you headed tonight?"

"Uh…" He runs a hand through his messy hair. "St. Louis? No—Colorado. I'm pretty sure."

I laugh. "I would make a joke about scrambling your brain, but with your travel schedule I don't think I should take credit."

"You did, though." He reaches across the sofa and squeezes my knee. "Can I take you out for a real date after we get back? And then, like, a dozen more of them?"

My heart stutters. That's a wonderful and also a terrible idea. I hadn't been kidding when I'd told James I met him at the wrong time. I don't want to jump into dating someone so quickly after Charles. "Well…"

James makes a stabbing motion toward his heart. "Okay, ow. How about *one* date, then? And no pressure."

"*Yes*," I agree. "Of course. In case you couldn't tell, I had a really good time with you last night. But—"

"But my timing sucks." He rubs a hand over his eyes. "I know. I was listening. I just didn't want to hear it." He drops his hand and stands up. "I'll walk you home."

"It's ten blocks, James. Every girl in Brooklyn can walk ten blocks without a safety detail. Except Delilah, I guess."

"That's just how I was raised." He shrugs. "I'll walk you home, unless you'd rather be alone." He reaches for my hand, and it feels so nice that I don't turn down his offer after all.

We head out into the crisp winter day, our coats zipped up and our hands still joined.

After a block in a companionable silence, he suddenly asks me a question. "Was it awful?"

"Um, what?" I ask. He *can't* mean the sex.

"The breakup," he says in a low voice. "After so many years, it has to be strange."

Oh. And here I'd avoided thinking about that for more than twelve hours.

I glance at him, and his gaze is everywhere but on me.

"It was somewhat awful," I admit. "Nobody expected me to break up with him. At first Charles didn't believe me. Then he got angry, which actually made things easier. If he'd been sad, I would've only felt guilt. But I didn't need a lecture from him about taking him for granted. And how I'd regret it."

James makes a sound of irritation, but otherwise holds his tongue.

"My mother isn't happy about it, either. She loves Charles."

"Is that because..." The sentence dies without a conclusion. "Because...?"

"Is he, uh, Chinese American, too? Is that a rude question?"

I laugh and shake my head. "It's not rude. But Charles is *Korean* American, so it's not really a cultural thing. My mom just likes his work ethic."

"That's a mom kind of thing," he guesses.

"Right. Or at least it's my mom's thing. But, God, work ethic isn't everything. Charles literally stays an hour after every other new hire in his office, every night. He chose the job over me a long time ago, and I'm just expected to nod along with it. I'm so tired of people who want to help me plan my future."

"Huh. I'd like to plan a few nights in your future," he mutters.

I crack up laughing. "Let me guess—there'd be some nakedness involved?"

"Well, *after* dinner," he says, and I laugh again. "But I know you need me to back off. I'll do that if you need me to. But just so you know, I want to date you. Last night wasn't just a hookup for me."

"Me neither," I say softly. "I like you. But this is a strange time for me."

"I know. And I hate that we're headed out on a road trip tonight," he says wistfully. "Can I call you tomorrow from... wherever?"

I laugh. "Sure. Maybe you'll figure out where the game is by then."

"Let's hope so. Although the team doesn't care, so long as I bring the visitor sweaters on the road. I'll probably get teased for leaving the bar with you last night."

"Oh boy." My face heats as I wonder how raunchy the locker room can get. "Will it be bad?"

"Nah. They go hard at each other but easy on me. It's poor sportsmanship to be a dick to the guy who makes less than a tenth as much as you do."

"It's nice that they realize that."

"Right?" He squeezes my hand. "Besides, if someone is an asshole, they risk payback. I might just forget their favorite color of tape or neglect to get the stink out of their pads."

I bark out a laugh. "You'd do that?"

He gives me a lopsided smile. "I'd be tempted."

I'm still laughing as I look up to cross the Avenue toward my apartment building. There's a man seated on the stoop, watching me, clutching a generous bouquet of roses.

It's Charles.

CHAPTER TWELVE

WHO IS
THAT?

12

Emily

Charles watches us approach, shock on his face.

James says, "Sweetheart, is that...?"

"Yes," I say tersely. I loosen my grip on his hand, because I'm not about to rub it in Charles's face.

James takes the hint and releases my hand, but not without running his index finger up my palm on the dismount. The boy has *moves*. "Should I go?" he asks quietly.

I stop and turn to him. "Probably." I can almost feel Charles's stare burning a hole through me.

"All right." His dark eyes are grave. "But we'll talk tomorrow morning. Take care of yourself, sweetheart." He leans in and gives me a kiss on the cheekbone. He shoots a look at Charles that I swear has the force of Trevi's slap shot.

Then he casually turns around and strolls back toward Midwood.

I take a deep, slow breath, peel my eyes off James's ass, and try to gather my wits.

Charles is already on his feet and pacing toward me. "Who is *that?*"

"A friend."

"A *friend,*" he repeats. "Emily!"

"What?" I gasp. "Don't ask, okay? Just don't."

His eyes dart in the direction where James's retreating form is probably still visible. And then he says something completely unexpected. "That's the guy who got the assist in the hockey game last night."

"Wait, what?" I sputter. "How did you know that?"

His head droops, and he looks down at the bouquet in his hands. "I was sitting at home watching the hockey game. I don't even know why, because you're the one who likes hockey. But there was this thing that happened—a guy got a goal right after the equipment manager handed him the stick. And I thought, 'Emily would think that was so cool.' And I just really missed you. So I called."

"Oh." *Hell.*

"You didn't answer my calls," Charles says, offering me the flowers. "And I ended up calling the land line kind of late. I was worried. But your mom said you were out."

I take the flowers, because he's just standing there holding them out to me. "You don't have to worry about me, Charles. I'm fine." This is so awkward. I hope I don't look as guilty as I feel right now, doing the walk of shame at noon on a Sunday.

"You met that guy *once*, I thought. What is happening right now?"

"We were friends. But Charles—this is really none of your business."

"Of course it is!" he thunders. "He's walking you home, and it's none of my business? We need to talk. I have things to say. I miss you. In spite of the hockey and the trouble we

126

were having. We don't love all the same things. But I still love you. And I'm sorry I didn't say that more often. I'm just...sorry."

My eyes begin to burn. I'd wanted to hear those words for a *long* time. "Thank you," I bite out.

"Can we go inside?" he asks. "I'd really like to spend some time with you. When you didn't answer me at all, I got seriously worried."

"Well..." I clear my throat. "Listen. These flowers are beautiful. And I really appreciate what you're saying. But we are not getting back together. I—"

"Jesus." He jerks back a few inches. "Can't we at least talk about it? You're just going to throw those years of our lives away?"

"No," I say sharply. "If you let me speak for a second, I could explain."

He snaps his mouth shut, but his expression says that he isn't looking forward to hearing me out.

"You were my first date. My first kiss, my first everything. And a lot of it was great—"

"Really great," he insists.

"I'm speaking now," I say firmly. He never did listen to me. But that isn't my biggest issue. "We take each other for granted, Charles. Not because we're terrible people. It's because we don't have any frame of reference. You're the only boyfriend I know. I'm the only girl you've dated. That's not okay with me anymore. I don't want to be the person you ended up with by default."

He flinches, probably because he can feel the unsaid part of that sentence—I don't want to end up with him by default, either. "You want more...experience dating?"

"Yes," I say, leaping at this opening. "I don't want to look back twenty years from now and wonder if I made the best choice or just the safe choice."

He bristles. "What if you look back in twenty years and wonder why you let me go?"

"That's a risk," I admit.

"But now you've met someone," he growls. "And he gets great hockey seats. So you're willing to toss me aside and have a little adventure? Did you even wait to break up with me? How long has this been going on?"

"Charles," I say in a low voice. "I have always been loyal to you. Don't make me regret that by questioning my morals. I don't deserve that."

He clamps his mouth shut again and scans my features, anger and uncertainty painted all over his face.

The truth is that I know this looks bad. I didn't mean to break up with Charles on a Sunday and hook up with James on the following Saturday. But I didn't do anything wrong. And I won't let him tell me I did.

"Look. You don't have to like it," I say quietly. "But I was honest with you last week when I said I couldn't be your girlfriend any longer. Be sad. Be angry if you need to be. But don't accuse me of going behind your back."

"I want us to go the distance," he insists, sounding miserable. "I want to give you everything. You said you wanted time alone. Don't date that guy."

"Charles." I suck in a breath. "I think you'd better go. There's nothing more I have to say right now."

He stares at me. Like he can't imagine that could be true. But I stare right back at him. Unwavering.

After a long moment, he steps past me and walks down the street in the direction of his apartment.

It takes me a second to snap out of it. I hurry inside the building.

The moment I get inside the apartment, my mother pounces. "Where *were* you last night?"

"Oh geez. Not you, too," I grumble.

"Charles was out of his mind," she says. "He's worried about you."

"That is his problem, not mine," I say firmly. "Seriously, Mom. I broke up with him, and he has got to let me go."

"He won't if he's smart," she returns, scrubbing our little dining table with a sponge. "You're perfect for him. You're the very best he can do."

I whirl around, surprised. "Thank you, I think. That's usually what you say to me about him."

"Also true," she sniffs.

I laugh out some of the tension in my chest. "It's over, Mom. Charles and I were in a rut so deep we couldn't see over the sides. I need to live a little. He could, too."

"But he works so hard," she points out.

"No kidding! But that's his *choice*. He works much harder at his job than he does at being with me."

My mother makes a *tsk tsk* sound and shakes her head. Her dark, glossy hair is sprinkled with gray. "Don't be short-sighted," she says. "Hard work builds character. Fun doesn't last."

I don't argue back, because there's really no point. I go into my room and shut my door, flopping onto the bed the same way I've been doing since we moved into this apartment fifteen years ago.

Now I'm alone with my thumping heart. I hate conflict. I hate fighting with Charles and defending myself to my mother. Closing my eyes, I picture James. His boyish smile.

His wavy hair, which is a different texture than mine. His sculpted arms flexing as he—

Okay, that daydream got hot and heavy fast.

I never intended to hop into bed with another man just a few days after my big breakup. And I'd felt sleazy running into Charles while holding James's hand. Like I'd done something wrong.

But I haven't. It's just hard to live your best life with other people judging. And I realize now that there were a lot of aspects to my relationship with Charles that I accepted without question.

I know better now. I also know I don't want a new relationship just yet. Not really.

But then there's James. What am I going to do about James?

CHAPTER THIRTEEN

YOU KNOW THIS FOR A FACT?

13

James

I'm in Seattle. The guys love it here, because the hotel is nice and the food is good. We lost our game in double overtime, but the team doesn't seem too broken up about it.

"One point instead'a two points," O'Doul had said. "We'll get the next one."

Now they're carousing in the hotel bar, happy as a flock of ducks in Prospect Park and twice as loud.

The only guy brooding over his phone is me. We fly back to New York on Saturday night after our game in Vegas, but Emily and I are having trouble finding a time to go out again. I can't help wondering if running into her lovelorn ex is the reason.

"Want to shoot pool?" Castro asks, nudging me in the elbow. "You can be on my team." He's been working pretty hard on his game lately.

"Is Heidi Jo our opponent?" I ask without looking up.

"Yeah."

"Then no."

"But Jimbo, buddy. Playing a great opponent is how you get good."

"Is it?" I grumble. "Not sure that always works."

"Wait," Castro says, turning on his barstool to face me. "Are we talking about pool right now? Or girls?"

"That second thing," I mumble. "She told me we met at the wrong time. And I brushed that aside, but maybe she's right. I can't even find a free night to take her out to dinner. In the meantime, her ex is showing up with flowers. Every day, probably."

"You know this for a fact?" Castro asks.

"Nah. I just got a feeling. He ignored her so bad she ditched his ass. But that guy is smart—college degree, good job on Wall Street. He probably realizes how bad he fucked up. He's probably rolling out the rug for her right now while I'm stuck here losing at pool with you."

Castro laughs. "So much negativity at such a young age."

He's a few years older than I am. At most.

"You're just sitting here psyching yourself out, aren't you? Just because you like this girl a lot, and your schedules are kind of a mess right now?"

"Maybe," I admit. "But who wants to date a guy who travels one hundred fifty nights a year?"

"She will, Jimbo. Give it a chance. Invite her to brunch if you can't find a night for dinner. Meet her for coffee. Just show her that you care, and the rest will work itself out."

"Hmm." I scrub a hand over my face. "Okay. Sure."

"Now can we lose at pool to my wife?"

"Nope." I set down my empty beer bottle. "Now I gotta call my girl and compare calendars. I'm gonna make this work."

"But *dude*. What about my needs?"

I slap him on the back and carry my phone out of the bar. I lean against a column in the lobby and text Emily goodnight. I'd call, but it's late in New York.

A second later, I'm delighted when she dials me right back. "James!" she says brightly when I answer. "Bummer about that overtime loss."

I smile to myself. "You watched?"

"I'm supposed to be doing research for a paper, but I kept checking the score."

"Uh-huh. And how's that paper coming along?"

"Slowly."

I laugh. "Is it due before the weekend? Because I'd really like to find a moment to see you."

"Sorry about Saturday and Sunday night. I don't usually have to work both of them, but my boss asked me to cover for somebody."

"I wouldn't have thought a college bookstore would even be open on Saturday night," I complain. "Who shops for books then?"

"The nerds of the world, James. Honestly, the place will be pretty dead. But they'll have me restocking the shelves. It's not just books, either. There are pens, stationery, office supplies, purple sweatshirts..."

"Wait. Purple? That's the NYU color?"

"Yes sir."

"And the Bruisers' team color."

"Right. This means I should be wearing my NYU garb to games."

"No, baby. This means something bigger than that. Two people, each with a closet full of purple clothing. It's *destiny*."

She giggles. "Must love purple. And hockey."

"I'd put hockey first, but sure." She laughs again, and the

sound of it melts me so much that I make a truly wild offer. And I hope I won't regret this. "Emily, what if you came over for Sunday dinner this weekend? We have it at two in the afternoon."

"With your family?"

"Yeah, and I'm honestly a little terrified to have you meet them. But I really want to see you. The food is really good, too. Just saying."

She's quiet for a second. "You want me to meet your family."

"My aunts and cousins," I clarify. "It doesn't have to be a huge big deal." I'm lying out of my ass right now because my aunt *will* try to make a big deal out of it. But that's on her. That woman loves drama.

"But I'm not an easy guest," she says slowly. "I don't want to offend anyone if I just eat the salad."

"Well, Sunday dinner has, like, a dozen dishes on the table. There will be pastas and vegetables and sides of all kinds. And, sure, a ham or something. But I'll just tell Aunt Luna that you don't eat red meat and she won't bat an eye. Swear to God."

"Okay," she says after a beat. "I'd love to come. What can I bring?"

"Just your pretty face," I say, my voice pure gravel, because I'm thinking about kissing her. "I'll pick you up at one thirty?"

"I'll walk over myself," she says. "And I'll see you on Sunday."

I tell her that I'll be counting the minutes, and we sign off.

And now I have to tell Aunt Luna that I'm bringing a guest on Sunday.

She's going to flip out.

Emily

I told myself that it was too soon to date anyone. Because it is.

Yet here I am, climbing the steps up to the front porch of James's auntie's three-story home, carrying a steamer basket full of three dozen chicken and cabbage dumplings that my mother and I made.

These dumplings are my absolute favorite thing in the world, and we hadn't made a batch in quite a long time.

But last night I'd confessed that I was going to a midday meal where I would meet the extended family of the man I'd just begun dating.

My mother's mouth had opened and closed several times in quick succession. "Where does he live?" she'd finally asked.

I'd seen the question for what it was—an attempt to figure out what sort of guy James is without seeming to pry. But neighborhoods can be very telling. Bensonhurst, for example, is home to a Chinese population along with quite a few Jews and Russians.

"He lives just over in Midwood. It's a big Italian family."

"Mmm," she'd said in another shocking display of discretion.

I'd almost laughed. "He's twenty-three years old, and he has a really neat job with the Brooklyn Bruisers hockey team. Which means he's on the road with them a lot of the time, and since I have to work tonight, Sunday afternoon is the only time this week I can see him."

"Hockey?" my mother had said, a pained expression on her face. "Don't they fight?"

"*He* doesn't, Mom. He's very sweet. With lovely manners. You might even like him."

She'd pursed her lips, and I'd braced myself for another lecture about Charles. "Is he a nice boy?" she'd asked.

"Yes," I'd responded immediately. "The night I had that allergic reaction, he drove me to the ER and hung around for three hours just because he didn't want to leave a woman alone in the middle of the night."

Her eyes had warmed, as if I'd just shown her a screenshot from the Panda cam we both haunt. "Then we had better make a good impression," she'd said.

Three dozen dumplings later, here I stand, ringing the doorbell.

When the door swings open a moment later, I can no longer remember why I didn't want to date James. Because there he is in all his burly, brown-eyed glory. He's opening the door and taking the bulky shopping bag from my hands and ushering me into a living room with shiny wood floors, curvy upholstered furniture with wooden feet, and accordion-folded window curtains.

"Come in, come in!" a round-faced woman with dancing eyes calls from the arched doorway to a distant, steamy kitchen. "I'm Luna, and you must be Emily!" Her wide-open smile suggests that she's either permanently happy or almost as tickled to meet me as the hockey players had been that night at the pizza place.

"It's lovely to meet you," I say. "My mother and I made some dumplings."

"Ooh! Wonderful. I love dumplings. Should we reheat them?" She barely takes a breath, gabbing as James hangs up my coat and carries the dumplings into the kitchen. "Are we steaming them or frying them?" She shuffles huge pots around a six-burner stove like a five-star chef.

"Steaming is fastest," I say.

"But fried dumplings are *divine*." She's already pulling a giant cast iron pan out of a cupboard and heaving it onto a burner.

Then? She heats up some oil and begins frying three dozen dumplings while talking my ear off. I hear all about her hairdresser's favorite recipe, about James's difficulties with the snowblower, and also about a taxicab accident on the next corner.

When she finally darts off to take a ham out of the oven, one of James's cousins—Tessa—turns the last few dumplings and takes over where Luna left off in the commentary.

"Okay, Tessie," James says, finally breaking in. "Maybe I could monopolize Emily for a second?" He puts a soda into my hand. "I wish I could say that dinner will be quieter, but that would be a lie."

I don't mind at all, though. The Carozza family is endlessly entertaining. James steers me away from Tessa, introducing me to three more cousins. Then his mother and father arrive, too, followed by an elderly man.

"Mom, Pops, this is Emily, the girl I told you about."

I shake their hands one at a time. Mr. Carozza looks like a rangier, older James. He gives me a friendly smile. Whatever differences he and his son have, they're not on display today.

"And this is Uncle Alberto, who is at least a hundred years old," James says.

"That is a lie," Uncle Alberto insists. "I only *feel* like it." He pats my arm. "Now let's eat a whole lot of lasagna, no?"

James leads me into a large formal dining room and pulls out my chair like a gentleman. He hadn't been kidding about this meal. No wonder he tries not to skip it—the table is laden with more hot dishes than I can count.

There is a brief moment of quiet while Uncle Alberto says a prayer, but the second he's done, Luna pipes up. "The meatless lasagna is the one in the blue pan!" she announces. "And I made my deviled eggs. Wait—can you eat eggs?"

"I absolutely can," I say. "Thank you for thinking of me."

Two minutes later, my plate is so full of food I can no longer remember what color the china pattern was. "I'm going to gain ten pounds today," I announce to James. "And I'm not even sorry."

He winks at me and gives my lower back a quick, affectionate rub. I love how comfortable he is in all this chaos. Before I met James, I hadn't known that calmness was sexy. But it is. He has a sturdy, peaceful way about him that I appreciate.

"So," Alberto says. "I got two questions for you, Emily."

"Oh boy," James says under his breath.

"In the first place, what is in these dumplings? They're *divine*."

"Thank you. They're chicken, cabbage, and scallions. The sauce is soy-based, with a touch of vinegar and some chili oil."

"You hear that, Luna? What a combination. We could put that in a ravioli."

"Who is the 'we' in this scenario?" Luna asks. "Do you mean me? Nobody likes a passive-aggressive man."

He doesn't even bother answering that query. "My other question—what are your intentions regarding my grandson?"

"He's not your grandson, he's your great nephew," Tessa argues.

"Well, I think he's pretty great," Alberto says with a shrug. "That's why I ask."

140

"Um…" I feel my face redden. It's a silly question, but I can't help but wonder how many people heard the story of James keeping Luna out of his apartment last weekend when I was in there. Naked.

"Don't tease her," James growls.

"Who says I'm teasing?" Alberto returns. "James wants to date you. He's been moping around here hoping you'll say yes. Like this." Alberto makes a droopy face like a sad basset hound, and his family erupts in laughter.

James puts his head in his hands. "I have not. Emily, ignore him."

"It's a fair question," I say, nudging his knee with mine. "And anyway, I've decided to date you. Because I don't think I can resist. Your family is too entertaining, for starters."

They all cheer, and James removes his red face from his hands and smiles at me.

I hold his gaze, even as the conversation moves on. "I wasn't teasing," I whisper. "I want to get to know you better."

"Aw, sweetheart." He leans in and gives me the quickest lip-touch of a kiss. "You are so brave to say that even after you met my family."

After dinner—and dessert and coffee—James and I take a walk around the neighborhood just for some peace and quiet. "When do you have to be at the stadium?" I ask him.

"Six." He checks the time. "I can walk you home, first."

"Okay," I say, deciding not to argue. I slip my hand into his, instead.

"But we have to go back to the house and get your… dumpling holders."

"Right," I agree, remembering the steamer baskets.

"And I have a ticket for Thursday's game, if you can make it."

"Really?" I perk up. "I'd love to try. I'll have to look at the work schedule."

"Awesome. It's not exactly a date, but—"

"—I *really* love hockey."

"Destiny," he says with a wink. We walk up the driveway together. "I have the ticket upstairs. Do you want me to run up and grab it?"

"I'll go, too. I don't mind the stairs." I step forward and start the climb.

He chuckles, following me. "All right. Just so you know, the ticket is real. This wasn't a ploy to get you up to my room."

When I reach the top, I turn around. "If you say so. But here we are."

"Here we are," he echoes, a cute, lopsided smile on his face. "Be a shame to waste it."

I step forward and slip my hands into his jacket, the invitation unmistakable.

He kisses me, and then he lets out a groan. "You kill me. You know that? I'm supposed to leave for work in half an hour."

"Better work fast, then," I say, moving toward the heat of his body, placing a palm over his steadily beating heart.

His next kiss is electric. And I regret nothing.

The End

ALSO BY SARINA BOWEN

MORE BROOKLYN HOCKEY!

Rookie Move (Leo & Georgia)

Hard Hitter (O'Doul & Ari)

Pipe Dreams (Beacon & Lauren)

Brooklynaire (Nate and Rebecca)

Overnight Sensation (Castro & Heidi Jo)

Superfan (Silas and Delilah)

Sure Shot (Bess and Tank)

Shenanigans (Charli & Drake)

And don't miss these players in their spin-off books:

Moonlighter (Eric Bayer & Alex)

Bountiful (Beringer & Zara)

COLLEGE HOCKEY

The Year We Fell Down #1

The Year We Hid Away #2

The Understatement of the Year #3

The Shameless Hour #4

The Fifteenth Minute #5

Extra Credit #6

CPSIA information can be obtained
at www.ICGtesting.com
Printed in the USA
LVHW091602120622
721092LV00004B/687
CPSIA information can be obtained
at www.ICGtesting.com
Printed in the USA
LVHW091602120622
721092LV00004B/687

9 781950 155347